About This Book

Nate is pulled into a mission to rescue a kidnapped woman, being held in Paris. But a normal mission versus one run by Terkel is a whole different story. Nate's first telepathic communication tells him that this will be like nothing else in his life.

During a layover in Paris, while traveling to start a job in Africa with Bullard, Madeline awoke, tied up in a strange hotel room with another female captive, named Anna. Nate comes to the rescue and shares how he had been called in to locate Madeline, when she didn't arrive as planned. Yet she wonders if she can trust him, especially when she has no recollection of who kidnapped her in the first place.

When Anna disappears again, Madeline's even more worried. What are the chances the kidnappers are looking for round two with Madeline as well?

Sign up to be notified of all Dale's releases here!
https://geni.us/DaleNews

Dale Mayer

TERK'S GUARDIANS
NATE 08

NATE: TERK'S GUARDIANS, BOOK 8
Beverly Dale Mayer
Valley Publishing Ltd.

ISBN-13: 978-1-778863-58-5
Print Edition

Books in This Series:

CHAPTER 1

T ERK SAT AT the table, his team growing and expanding by the week, it seemed. He needed to get one of those big-screen TVs, like what Ice had set up in her place for their team. It would be great for conference calls or Zoom meetings. He reached for his phone, selected a Contact to call, and put the phone on Speaker. "Riff, what's going on?" Terk asked. "I thought you were coming back with Sanders and Ania."

"They'll be there today," he replied, "but I got another lead on my fiancée, so I'm taking off to do that." He hesitated a bit and asked carefully, "You don't have a job, do you?"

"I do, but it depends on where you're heading."

"To the US. The state of Maine to be exact. I need to talk to an old friend of hers. Apparently she spoke to him not too long before she died."

"You could call," Terk suggested.

"I know I could, but he's an old guy, not big on technology, and really not big on strangers. Plus, he seems to have a chip on his shoulder about me."

"Ah. Do you want backup?"

"No, this won't be anything physical," Riff stated, "but I'll be over there. If you've got anything you need me to do while I'm there, you can let me know. I'm always available, but you guys could probably use some peace and quiet for a while."

"That's not likely to happen for quite some time," Terk declared, with a note of humor in his tone. "You know what the world is like."

"Yeah, it's a mess, and I'm damn tired of it."

"I hear you there," Terk murmured. "Who knows whether we'll get any calls for assistance or not, but, maybe after you're done, depending on whatever's going on, we'll move you to the next job."

"What's that?"

Just then Gage walked in, holding up his phone. "Bullard's been trying to get through to you, but it keeps ringing busy, so he called me instead."

"Hang on a minute, Riff," Terk said, turning to Gage and taking the phone from his hand. "Bullard, you still there?"

"Yeah, I am. I had a new nurse I was bringing over to see if she wanted to do some training here. She landed in Paris and was due to get a connecting flight after spending two days there, but she apparently missed the flight. I checked the hotel, and there's no sign of her. I want to send a man over, but I'm spread pretty thin at the moment."

"That's fine. I've got some men who are available, and we are closer," Terk pointed out. "Is this a case of needing our particular brand of skills or just manpower?"

"I don't know yet," Bullard admitted. "One of the reasons why I was looking at hiring her is because she has a reputation for uncanny healing." He sounded almost lost in thought. "Although that's not necessarily a *your group versus my group* thing, I just thought I would check and see if she happened to have some abilities. You know how we could always use that here," he muttered. "Yet it seems that, as soon as anybody finds out about your group, they head to you." He sounded frustrated. "I don't care whether she goes to you or to me. I just want to know that somebody I feel responsible for is safe, and, so far, I haven't been able to raise her at all. We've done some basic research, so I'll send you the file. If you can give us a hand on this one, I would appreciate it."

"We got it," Terk replied. "Riff is heading to the US right now, so that won't work, but I do have somebody else I was looking at hiring, or at least at testing, so this might be a good opportunity for that."

"How about I send one of my guys as backup?"

"Sounds good."

"So you have another new guy who's doing your work?"

"Maybe," Terk said. "He's not admitting to doing this energy work, but he's an ex-Navy SEAL who's been working out of Ireland for the last four years. I heard via the grapevine that he had some abilities. He's not against doing a job for me, but he certainly isn't being forthcoming about any unique skills I might be interested in."

"Of course not." Bullard laughed. "Nobody would because it'll make him sound crazy. So, give him the intel on the nurse I lost in Paris."

"I'll contact Nate and set it up. Send the file. We're on it."

CHAPTER 2

N ATE WORTHINGTON PUT away his phone and turned to look up at the quickly changing schedule of flights on the board ahead of him. Most of the flights were delayed now, compared to just ten minutes ago when he had last looked. Seemed Bullard's man, Garret, was having the same problem, but he would get here when he got here.

As Nate stared out the window, he could see the weather worsening, which wouldn't help a woman lost in Paris. He walked up to the customer service desk but ground to a halt suddenly, feeling an odd sensation, as if he were being watched. He turned ever-so-slowly and looked around at all the travelers milling about, disgusted due to the changes in the upcoming flights. Yet Nate knew that singular gaze homing in on him had nothing to do with any of these tourists. He stilled and opened his senses slightly.

The gaze remained intense.

Moving carefully, trying not to obviously track this new presence, Nate straightened and looked around casually, noting people still gathered close by. However, this particular energy focused on Nate came from farther away and off to the side. He lifted his gaze over the sea of heads and latched on to a man standing at the edge of the crowd, whose gaze now locked on to Nate's. The stranger gave a slight incline of his chin in acknowledgment, and then, as if the crowd sensed something going on, it dispersed suddenly. Nate walked toward the man standing there, studying him carefully. Large, powerful, and fairly taciturn, the stranger watched Nate approach.

"I'm Brody. Terkel sent me."

In those few words, he had apparently conveyed all he planned on saying. He motioned to the exit, as if to say, *Come with me.* Nate hesitated, but Brody didn't even pause to look back, just took off.

Nate caught up with him outside. "Where are we going? The flights are that way."

"Your flight's been canceled," Brody stated. "Since time is of the essence, we'll take a private plane."

"Yet these flights were canceled due to bad weather, which remains a threat," Nate shared, while studying this man who appeared to have picked him out of the crowd.

"We can get around that."

Nate's eyebrows shot up at that. "Don't tell me. Terkel's got somebody who can control the weather now?"

Brody broke character and chuckled. "No, but, man, I wish we could. That would be a helpful scenario." He appeared amused.

"Maybe, but if anybody ever found out …"

"That's always the problem, isn't it?" he muttered. "The more people who find out what we can do, the more problems we have."

"You seem to be totally okay talking about it."

"Only with people who are the same as me." When Nate frowned at that, Brody snorted. "Don't bother denying it. I can sense powerful energy just as much as you can. You knew I was watching you. You just didn't know who I was."

"I'm still not sure I know who you are."

"Brody," he stated, for the second time. "That's all you need to know right now."

Nate wasn't sure Brody was correct about that, but it was all Nate would get at the moment. So Nate followed Brody onto the tarmac, then down and around, away from the crowds, even passing equipment stalls, before they came to a private hangar, where a small plane idled.

The pilot stood there atop the steps, his arms crossed, his foot tapping impatiently.

Brody nodded. "I gather we were supposed to leave a while ago."

"Yeah, the sooner, the better," the pilot noted.

"It took me a bit to find you," Brody shared.

"If you'd let me know you were looking," the pilot replied, his tone mild, "it would have been easier."

"Yeah," Brody noted, "but it doesn't always happen that way."

Not sure what to do with that exchange of information, Nate remained quiet yet in step with Brody, wondering at an operation like this that had private planes on hand. "Does Terkel always commandeer flights to make his stuff happen?"

"When lives are at stake, yes," Brody stated, now on board, waving Nate to a seat. "Sit down. I need to talk to the pilot."

Nate's eyebrows kicked up at the order, something he wasn't used to. Yet he took a seat, pondering the sudden turn of events. He had told Terkel that he would make his way over to France as soon as he could. But apparently that wasn't fast enough. Nate's phone rang just then, and he looked down to see Terkel's number. "Are you always this impatient?" he asked, right off the bat.

"No, but, in this case, this young woman came to do a

job to help a friend of mine. When she didn't show up and remains missing, we're very concerned about her well-being."

"Of course," Nate agreed, with a nod. "That is why we're here, after all. I didn't know you needed me now."

"It's always a case of we need you now," Terkel replied, humor entering his tone. "The good news is that you have Brody, and he'll show you the ropes."

"Sure," Nate noted, shaking his head. "Do you want to tell me who this Brody is though?"

"You could ask him yourself," Terkel stated.

"Yeah, I'm pretty sure I'll get shut down over that one. Is everybody on your team this unfriendly?"

Terk started to chuckle. "Brody has good reason to be as suspicious of you as you are of him," Terk shared. "So a little trust would go a long way in this instance. Maybe you guys should talk to each other."

"Maybe," Nate muttered, "but it takes two to talk." And, with that, he ended Terkel's call, which gave him some measure of satisfaction. After all, Terkel had rearranged Nate's world just now without seeming to give a crap about contacting him and letting him know. Communication was big as far as Nate was concerned, and it was hard to work for people who didn't understand that.

Almost immediately his brain rattled, and a hard knocking sound followed.

Nate shuddered at the pain, and just then a hand grabbed him by the shoulder. He looked up to see Brody standing there, glaring at him.

"Open the damn door," Brody declared. "There's stubbornness, and then there's stubbornness."

Nate blinked several times, then mentally heard the *click* of a door opening, and Terkel's voice slammed into Nate's brain. Nate shuddered at the onslaught. "Turn down the damn volume," he cried out loud.

Immediately the volume eased. *Now that you've opened up some telepathic communication, we can more easily reach you,* Terkel muttered. *Keep that damn door open, at least as much as we need to share our thoughts with each other.* And, with that, Terk was gone just as quickly as he came.

Nate tried to blink away the pain, as Brody took a seat opposite him in the small plane. Nate wasn't sure what had just happened. Yet he looked up when Brody spoke.

"Resistance is futile." And then he laughed as if it were the funniest joke on earth.

Nate glared at him. "I still don't quite understand what the hell that was."

"Yet you do understand," he countered. "You're definitely in the power grid, the same as I am. You're probably just not used to being around other energy workers who are just as powerful as you. Or, in Terkel's case, way-the-hell more powerful. We'll need whatever rest we can get, so grab it now." With that, Brody closed his eyes, shutting out all opportunity for more conversation.

Sleep wasn't easy after what Nate had just experienced, plus his jaw wanted to drop open in shock over the painful telepathy. At the very least he wanted answers. He needed somebody to tell him something.

However, based on this most recent turn of events, he was pretty sure these people thought Nate could figure it out on his own. Truth be told, he probably could. He just didn't know if he could do it fast enough for this bunch. He felt very much as if he were being graded on a cut-and-dried scale of either pass or fail, and his future depended on it.

BRODY SNAPPED AT Terkel. *He's confused as all hell.*

That's not a problem, Terkel replied, his voice calm as ever.

Sometimes Brody wondered if Terk was normal at all, but they'd been brothers in many ways for so long that Brody never doubted anything this man said or did. Terk always seemed to have such a sense of control that it blew Brody away. On the other hand, Brody felt as if half the time Terk was completely silent or ready to snap at somebody.

It's all just energy. Remember that you're still coming back online, still healing, Terkel muttered. *You've been one of the last to surface, yet you expect yourself to be up and healing faster than everybody else.*

I should be, he growled.

You mean because of Clary? Sure, but she's also had her energies pulled in a million directions, Terkel noted. *So, what is he doing right now?*

Staring out the window as if his world just blew up.

It did. I didn't have time to be gentle about opening that door.

No, and you certainly were effective. It's open, but I can feel his thoughts spinning around, as he's trying to sort through what just happened.

Terkel sighed. *How bad is it? Do you think I need to go in and assess his abilities?*

No, I think he'll be just fine. A part of him remains quite pissed at the whole thing though.

Terkel laughed. *Yeah, being pissed is a whole lot better than a lot of other things he could be, so I'm not upset about that. You've been running on less sleep than normal, so I suggest you crash while you can. Grab a few hours before you land in the middle of whatever madness awaits you.*

I'm working on it, but we're about to head into a spot of ugly weather.

You'll be fine, Terkel replied, his voice reassuring. *Sleep, and by the time you wake up, you'll already be landing.*

Miffed, Brody didn't believe him. He stepped back out of the conversation, closed his eyes, opened them one more time to check on Nate, who still stared out the window. Brody took a moment to consider whether to let Nate be, and then, deciding against it, he sent him a direct order. *Sleep. It will be easier to deal with it afterward.*

Startled, Nate looked over at him. *Are you sure?*

I am, he declared, plain and simple. *We may have been a little rough in opening that door, but now that it's open, your world will only improve.*

With that, Brody closed his eyes, a smile on his lips, and let sleep overtake him.

MADELINE OPENED HER eyes, then stared around at what appeared to be a hotel room. She was lying on the bed, her hands bound behind her, her feet bound too. Panic set in, only to soon still, as energy washed though her, calming her emotions. Another woman was in the bed at her side. She appeared to be asleep, yet maybe not so much. Madeline studied her roommate carefully, quickly realizing that she was hurting. Madeline instinctively sent healing energy to ease her roommate's pain.

A few minutes later the other woman moaned and slowly opened her eyes. Then, as if on cue, she panicked as she realized she was also tied up. She tried to twist and get free or at least to be more comfortable, while she cried in muted sobs.

Madeline hated that awakening, that sense of violation and panic, knowing that you were in somebody else's control, a victim of circumstances. She whispered to her roommate, "It's okay. Take it easy."

The woman fell back to the bed and shifted, so she could see Madeline. "Oh my God," she muttered in a panicked voice. "Are we prisoners?"

Madeline nodded. "We are. I just don't know why."

"Neither do I," she cried out, now in a full-blown panic. "I didn't do anything." The woman's eyes filled with tears, and she whispered, "God, my head hurts."

"If you can go back to sleep, it would help," Madeline suggested, her voice low and reassuring. Of course she could also help her more easily if she were asleep or compliant. Right now she was too rattled to do anything to help her.

The other woman gave her a horrified look. "Sleep? Are you kidding?" she asked, her voice rising.

"*Shh*," Madeline whispered in a harsh tone. "We don't want to bring them back."

The other woman's crying cut off abruptly, and she gulped hard. "Do we know what they want?" she whispered.

"Not yet," Madeline murmured. "What's your name?"

She swallowed and then said, "Anna."

"I'm Madeline. If you're calm enough to talk to me, maybe we can figure out why we were selected for this."

"Selected?" Anna gave her a disgusted look. "Do you think we were … picked for this?"

"Do you see anybody else here?" At Madeline's frantic look around the empty room, she answered her own question. "It's just the two of us, as far as I've been able to sort out, and, if that's the case, why? What is it about us? What do they want from us, for us, because of us, or whatever?"

"I don't know," Anna muttered, staring at her blankly. "I was heading to the coffee shop to meet some friends," she shared.

"So where do you work?"

"At a law firm. We do divorces. I can't think of any cases that would require a kidnapping."

"I don't know about that," Madeline disagreed, with an attempt at humor. "A lot of divorces get pretty ugly."

"That they do. I'll give you that," Anna agreed, "but I've never come across one that involved this. Why us?"

"That's what I'm trying to figure out," Madeline replied. "Why us? Why not men? Why not somebody else sitting at the coffee shop?"

"I'm not sure I made it to the coffee shop," Anna noted, frowning. "My head's pretty fuzzy on that yet."

"Considering you have a headache, we were drugged or we were knocked out. Maybe both."

Anna winced. "I don't handle drugs very well anyway. I tend to react badly to them. So, if they drugged me, that would probably account for the headache, plus, I slept longer than you, right?"

Madeline nodded. "I've been awake for about half an hour, and, in that time, I haven't seen anybody."

Anna let out her breath and asked in a harsh whisper, "Is that a good thing?"

"I don't know. I would like to think we would get answers if someone came in, but even getting answers may not help us get out of here."

Anna shuddered. "I have to get out of here." She looked

around frantically. "Have you tried to escape?"

"No, I sure haven't," Madeline replied, with a note of humor. "Remember that part about I woke up just half an hour before you? Not to mention that you weren't awake yet, and I was hoping you might have some answers."

Anna collapsed back onto the bed, her head hitting the pillow, her eyelids closing with despair. "I don't have any ideas or answers."

"I'm a tourist in Paris really. I was in between flights, heading to Africa to work for a while," she shared, lost in thought, "so I really don't have a clue why I'm here."

"What do you do for a living?"

"I'm a nurse."

Anna blinked. "It doesn't sound as if we have anything in common at all. I live in Paris. So do you remember leaving the airport?"

"I did. I was booked into a hotel, and I ..." Madeline tried to focus her glazed eyes. "I had a two-day layover. I left the airport and took a bus to go to a coffee shop. I don't know that I made it there either."

"But if our intentions were to go to coffee shops, what are the chances that has something to do with our kidnappings?" Anna stared at Madeline.

"Going to a coffee shop is a very common thing," she replied. "It doesn't make any sense that it would have made us targets."

"No, but, sometimes in France, coffee shops have become quite a target themselves." Anna's own words made the color disappear from her face. "That is unfortunately true here."

"How would you have gotten there? Where do you live?" Madeline asked.

Anna paused. "I live on the other side of town from that particular coffee shop, but I was at my boyfriend's," she explained, her awareness seemingly coming back. "I spent the night with him."

"Okay, and where does he live?" Madeline asked.

"He's close to the airport," Anna replied. "I took the public transport route."

"I wonder if we were on the same bus?"

Anna stared at her. "Maybe. Especially if you were taking the one going downtown from the airport because you had a few hours to kill. If that were the case, it would make perfect sense because that's the one everybody uses."

Madeline nodded. "I had a two-day layover, so I had a hotel lined up. I was planning to stop for coffee on the way there. So, in theory, that could have put us on the same bus."

"But why would anybody care about us?" Anna asked, staring at her.

"I don't know, but that's the next thing we'll have to figure out. If we were picked up from the same location, that would be a start." Madeline was trying her best to think and to not panic at the same time. "I wonder if we were targeted because we're young females, though that's the last thing either one of us wants to consider, I'm sure." At the frightened look on Anna's face, Madeline shook her head. "No point in focusing on that."

Anna relaxed ever-so-slightly. "No, but, with just the two of us here, … I wish I remembered more, I don't recall very much. I just don't understand how we got here or how it all happened so quickly," she murmured.

Madeline continued to contemplate the whole scenario and frowned. She was unsure whether to say it out loud and shook her head. "Something happened on the bus. I didn't understand it, but I don't speak French," she admitted, "A conversation was going on behind me. I remember turning to look at them because of the anger that seemed to be increasing between them."

"And?" Anna stared at her. "What does that mean?"

Madeline frowned. "I don't know. I guess I'm wondering if I overhead something I shouldn't have. The stupid thing is, I don't speak French. So, whatever I had heard or whatever they think I'd heard, I don't know what it is anyway."

Anna gave a half laugh. "You're saying that this is a case of mistaken identity?"

"Not exactly." Madeline shrugged, then winced as the movement pulled at her shoulders painfully. "I'm just wondering if that has anything to do with it. Other than that, I'm not sure what else it could it be or why they would care."

"I don't know," Anna cried out, letting her own frustration boil over. "I haven't seen anybody but you since I woke up, and I don't know what's happening. So, if you're looking to me for answers, … don't bother. I don't have any."

Madeline took a slow, deep breath.

"Look. I'm sorry," Anna said. "I didn't mean to jump all over you. Obviously you're as much a victim here as I am, and it's just very distressing to realize this mess we're in."

"Yeah, you're not kidding. All I was doing was trying to catch a plane to a new job. Now I won't even have that waiting for me."

"But, if they understand what happened, surely the job will still be there when you get out of here."

"Maybe, I don't know. I was hesitant about accepting it in the first place. Now it seems as if somebody had other plans for me," she noted, with a hard laugh. "Not what I had in mind at all."

"No, of course not," Anna muttered.

Just then the hotel room door opened, jolting both women. An unmasked man came in, stared at both of them, and frowned. "Of all the stupid-ass things they have ever done, this is probably the stupidest."

Madeline blinked. "I'm sorry, but does that mean you'll let us go?"

He turned to her. "English?"

She nodded slowly. "Yes, I don't speak French, so I'm not sure what is going on here."

"You don't speak French?" he asked pointedly.

She shook her head, "No, I don't. Should I?"

He turned his gaze to Anna. "Do you?"

"Yes, I speak French. I live in Paris, but I'm not sure what difference it makes."

"Maybe none, maybe everything," He ran his hands through his hair, his frustration obviously eating away at him. "I still don't quite understand what happened here myself," he stated in a calm tone, which was still threatening as hell. "But I can tell you that I'm hoping to get this dealt with as quickly as possible." And, with that vague statement, he started to leave.

Madeline cried out, "Excuse me. I really need a bathroom."

He stared at her for a moment, then groaned. "Sure you do," he muttered, looking at the ceiling. "God damn it all." He walked over and jerked her to her feet.

She cried out over the roughness and the tingling sensations in her feet and hands, both which didn't seem to work immediately.

He winced. "Sorry. I'm sorry. I didn't mean that to be quite so rough."

He released her hands and feet and led her to the small en suite bathroom. As soon as she was done, her hands still wet from washing, she opened the door to find Anna standing in line. Madeline stepped out of the way, so Anna could enter the bathroom. Madeline spoke to the man, almost pleading, "I know that you'll take off and leave us," she began, as she cowered under his stare, "but is it possible to get a bottle of water or something to drink?"

He seemed to consider her request and then shrugged. "I'll see. I don't really know what'll happen to you at this point."

She didn't say anything, just nodded, not wanting to further upset him. She returned to her bed, but, instead of lying down, she sat up against the wall, hoping he would forget to tie their hands and feet again.

When Anna exited the bathroom, she followed suit, so they both now leaned against the wall.

He studied them for a moment, then turned to leave. "I'll be back in a bit." As he headed out, he locked the door.

Madeline sighed in relief, at least temporarily. "We're not exactly any wiser after that visit, but he didn't appear to want to hurt us."

"Right, and that's good news."

"Are your hands and feet still tingling?" At Anna's nod, Madeline asked her, "Can you run, you think?"

Anna frowned, shaking her head. "Ask me again in a few minutes."

"I think we've been tied up longer than we think. Otherwise our feet and hands wouldn't be so numb." That thought alone worried Madeline.

"I just wish I knew what was going on here," Anna wailed. "If we were both taken off the same bus, what are the chances that our visitor was talking to someone else on the bus, and now he worries that we overheard something we shouldn't have?"

"Maybe," Madeline agreed.

Anna grimaced. "In that case, I probably should have told him that I don't speak French, but it's obvious I do. My accent is a dead giveaway regardless."

"It's probably better to be truthful," Madeline noted, "but let's not volunteer any information that we don't have to."

"That makes sense too," Anna murmured. "My head is still killing me. I think it must be the drugs that we were given."

"That could very well be, and maybe that was a quick impulse on their part."

"I find myself wondering why they didn't just dump us somewhere."

"Maybe that's still what they're planning," Madeline suggested, looking over at her. "I got the impression that they don't quite know what to do with us. It sounds as if somebody made the decision to snatch us without the other party agreeing, and now they have to decide what to do with us."

"But if somebody decided to snatch us because he thought we were a danger to them and knew too much or whatever," Anna stated, looking over at Madeline, fear etched on her face, "chances are he'll win in terms of the decision-making."

"Let's not go there," Madeline noted. "If you were planning to meet your friends at that coffee shop, and you never showed, hopefully someone sent out an alert on you. Though, if anything major has happened in terms of something citywide, then that will probably overshadow your missing person's notice. So finding you could take a little longer."

When Anna didn't look convinced, Madeline continued. "It'll be obvious to my African contact that I didn't make it. Inquiries will be made, and definitely people will be looking for me."

"Sure, for a little while," Anna conceded, "and then very quickly we'll fall off the front page and become yet another cold case in the missing persons' files."

Madeline stared at her. "That's not the way we need to go in terms of attitude," she muttered. "We have enough to deal with here, so we need to keep our heads in the game and not borrow trouble."

"All I know is that I'm too young to die, and anything else they've got planned for us isn't something to look forward to either. So I don't see a silver lining."

Of course the alternative could be pretty ugly, and Madeline wasn't at all impressed with that concept either, but she didn't want to focus on it. She didn't want to focus on any of it. "He did lock the door, but is a guard posted outside? What are the chances that they just decide not to come back? Maybe they chose to not deal with us at all?"

"That would be a best-case scenario," Anna said, eyeing her. "Do you really think they'll do that?"

"I don't know what they'll do," Madeline admitted. "However, we've seen that one man's face, and that is concerning. If they had blindfolded us, we would have had a chance of being let loose, but I'm not so sure now."

"Yet," Anna argued, "if you think about it, if only one

person has seen us, then only one person is in danger of getting caught or us saying anything about him. Therefore, what's to stop them from taking him out and cleaning us up?"

Madeline sighed. "He's definitely a liability now to the other kidnappers."

"I wonder if he has any idea that he's been set up that way."

"I don't think he's that stupid. Yet he didn't seem to be too bothered about our situation, like they have done this before. Still, I'm not sure he thought that far ahead," Madeline shared. "You can bet somebody in the kidnapping group is thinking about it though. And they're making assessments right now as to the value of each person in-volved. Chances are good that nobody will come out of this in a good way."

"Good," Anna cried out. "I don't have any sympathy for anybody involved in kidnapping us."

"Yet it's likely that most of them weren't involved," she reminded her. "We don't know how many kidnappers there are, but it appears that somebody made the decision to take us, and other people will have to pay the consequences. Us too."

"Isn't life like that?" Anna asked, her voice fading, as her hands went to her head. "Seems we're always caught up in the fallout from other people's shitty decisions."

"Sometimes," Madeline murmured. "Close your eyes and rest. You'll surely wake up if he comes in again."

Anna shuddered but asked her, "You won't leave me alone, will you?"

"No, not at all. Should I find a way out of here," she added, with an eye roll, "I'll wake you up and take you with me. I promise."

Anna stared at her, as if assessing her character in this regard for a moment, and then nodded. "Yes, please," she muttered. "I think right now my greatest nightmare is to wake up and to find out I'm 100 percent alone."

"Not to worry," Madeline replied. "That's not who I am."

And, with that, Anna shut her eyelids and drifted off to an uneasy sleep.

CHAPTER 3

MADELINE OPENED HER eyes a while later, having drifted off herself. The two women were still alone, still hands-free, as Anna slept restlessly. Madeline got up, tested the viability of her feet, walked over to the window, and pulled back the curtain to look outside. For all intents and purposes, it seemed they were in a hotel. Traffic was down below but in the distance.

From what she could see, many parking lots surrounded the building she was in. Madeline had no way to contact anybody—no phone, no laptop, no money, nothing. Their room included a bathroom, and being left with their hands and feet free meant that they could use it as needed. She headed to the bathroom and gave her face a good scrub and pulled her fingers through her hair, trying to detangle some of the knots, before going back into the hotel room. She studied everything around her to determine where they were, what building they were in. She assumed they were still in France, but she had no proof of that.

As she sat down once again, Anna shifted in bed and woke up uneasily. When she realized where she was again, her eyes opened wide, and then she started to cry. "I was hoping it was a bad dream."

Madeline drew near and gave her a hug. "Sorry, but we're still here, and we have no idea how and, more important, why."

Just then came a knock on the door.

Madeline called out, "Hello? Who's there?"

The woman on the other side of the door replied, "Housekeeping, ma'am."

"Yes, yes, of course, come in, please."

But, when she tried the door, it was locked.

"Can you use your key?" Madeline asked. "I can't get to the door."

"Yes, certainly." The employee unlocked the door and pushed it wide open to get her cart inside.

Madeline stood and pulled Anna to her feet. Grabbing Anna's hand, Madeline smiled at the housekeeper. "Thank you so much. We'll just step out while you do your cleaning." Madeline quickly exited the room and, with Anna in tow, dragged her to the closest elevator, where they headed downstairs.

Anna gripped Madeline's hand tightly as she whispered, "Do you think they'll just let us go?"

"I don't know if our kidnappers were expecting housekeeping to arrive or if they just decided that we weren't worth the trouble."

Anna frowned at Madeline, then slowly nodded. "That would be huge."

As soon as they made it to the ground floor, Madeline and Anna stared at each other hesitantly, frozen in the elevator hallway.

Madeline broke their silence. "I know you probably want to run, but I think we should call the cops, give them our statements."

Anna immediately shook her head. "I don't want anything to do with the cops," she cried out. "No way."

"What if our kidnappers are picking up other women they've taken and expect to come back to get us now? They will be upset that we've escaped."

With horror, Anna shook her head over and over again. "More reasons to run away."

"And yet," Madeline added, squeezing Anna's hand, "you may not want to acknowledge it, but it is most certainly possible. It is possible," she repeated, as if to assure both of them.

"No, it's not," Anna argued. "They've let us go. No reason for them to come back after us now."

"Maybe not," Madeline conceded, "but I don't want to take a chance."

"No, I refuse to talk to the police." With that, Anna took one last look around the hotel and shuddered. "I don't want to be here another minute," she declared, pulling her hand from Madeline's grip. "Goodbye." And, with that, she bolted to the front door and outside.

That might be fine for Anna, as she lived in Paris, but, for Madeline—who didn't have her purse, her phone, even her passport was gone—she had nothing but the clothes she wore. She walked to the front desk and asked if she could use a phone, until she got a new one. The manager gave her one of the house phones, which she couldn't take any farther than the counter, and told her how to dial out. She didn't remember Bullard's number correctly, but, by the time she went through the operator a couple times, Madeline ended up getting him.

When he came on the phone, the anxiousness in his voice reassured her that he'd been out looking for her.

"Hey," she greeted him. "I'm not sure what's going on, but, yes, I was kidnapped."

At that, the hotel employee turned and looked at her, a little too quickly.

She lowered her voice and turned away to keep the desk clerk from hearing anything further. "But I have no passport, no money, and no place to stay." Then she quickly explained all that she could remember.

"Good God," Bullard replied. "Why would they do that?"

"I don't know," she murmured. "All I can tell you is that I can't go anywhere, and I hate to ask, but I'll need a hand."

"No problem," he stated. "I've got some men coming for you, but we didn't know where you were. Thankfully the two men coming to help you are capable of handling this."

"Where are they now?" she asked, instinctively turning to look around her.

"Is there a coffee shop in the hotel?"

"Yes," she said, "but I can't stay here, considering this is the place where we woke up, where the kidnappers will look for us here."

"Right. Give me a moment to contact the guys."

"You need to do it fast because I'm on a borrowed phone, and I'm afraid a hotel employee may take it back at any moment."

"Okay, I've got your GPS location. So stay in the lobby. You may need to wait, as the guys are about twenty minutes out."

"I think I can manage another twenty minutes," she told him, followed by a nervous laugh. "I'm not exactly in the best of shape."

"Are you hurt?" Bullard asked instinctively, his voice hard.

"No, they didn't hurt me or the other woman."

"Another woman was involved?" he asked, his voice rising.

"She just bolted. Once we got out of there, she freaked and ran. She's a local, so she had a place to go, but I don't have that luxury."

"No, but you can go to the coffee shop in the lobby and get a cup of coffee and something to eat while you wait," Bullard suggested. "I promise somebody will be there for you shortly and can pay your food bill."

"And if the kidnappers come back first?" she asked, quivering at the thought.

Bullard swore into the phone. "How about you just stay right there beside the front desk, until my men get there? Try to stay on this line as long as the desk clerk lets you."

She contemplated that for a moment, still feeling like a sitting duck. "How will I know that they are your men looking for me?"

"One is called Brody, and the other is Nate," he replied, as he gave her a physical description of each man. "Watch for two men, capable of taking on the world and laughing at the trouble."

"They better be ready," she said shakily, "because I don't think I can do too much more of this. Outside of going to the police or maybe the consulate here, I don't know what I'm supposed to do. I have nothing with me."

"We can fix this. Meanwhile you need to sit down. I worry about you going into shock."

She turned and looked around. "I guess I can sit in the lobby."

"At least that way, if your kidnappers come back and try to grab you, there will hopefully be a lobby full of people to help you," he explained. "Just remember that Brody and

Nate are on their way to get you and by now are probably about fifteen minutes out."

"Okay," she muttered. "I guess I have to hang up now." Hating to get off the phone, to lose that connection to Bullard, she ended the call and pushed the phone back over to the clerk and whispered, "Thank you." At his sharp look, she headed toward the lobby chair in full view of everything. She could only hope that her rescuers were coming in a hurry. She felt as if everybody was looking at her, judging her, or at least trying to assess what the hell was going on.

She couldn't even imagine how this would end up, but she didn't want anybody else to wind up in the same position she had just been in. Finally collapsing into the chair, her fingers tapping on the wooden frame, she sat here and waited.

NATE DROVE AS fast as the traffic would allow. When Brody's phone rang, he put it on Speaker. "Bullard, what's up?"

"Madeline just called me," he stated, his tone hard. "She'd been kidnapped, and she woke up in a hotel with somebody else, another woman who'd been kidnapped too. Madeline's sitting in the lobby right now, and they've taken her passport, her ID, her phone, everything. I've texted her location to you." He let out a harsh breath. "She's pretty shaken up, as you can imagine. I don't have the full details, but I'm much more concerned about your getting to her before her kidnappers return. Apparently the cleaning lady came in, and they got out that way."

"Good God." Brody punched her location into his

phone and got the street address, now giving turn-by-turn directions to Nate. "Okay, we're about ten minutes out," Brody told both Bullard and Nate.

Nate punched down on the gas pedal, racing toward the center of town.

Bullard sighed. "Good, although you'll still be later than I told her. I just need to know that she'll be there when you arrive."

"Yeah, us too. Meanwhile, can you phone the hotel and have them keep an eye on her until we get there?"

"Shit." Bullard groaned. "I should have thought of that." And, with that, he disconnected.

Nate looked over at Brody. "So, the case is done before it even started?"

"No, I don't think so." Brody shook his head. "This is not normal behavior."

"Yet if it was a mistake …"

"We'll have to get the full story from her, or as much as she knows anyway," Brody suggested, "but, if she's already pretty stressed, it might take a bit."

"It might," Nate agreed. "On the other hand she had the wherewithal to get a hold of Bullard, so that says a lot about her frame of mind."

"It does."

Nate asked, "What's this about another woman?"

"Apparently another woman was kidnapped with Madeline, but she's gone, didn't want to stick around to report it to the locals."

The thought of kidnapping two women just reminded Nate how often so much of the work he'd done in this world had a component of unintended consequences. Things frequently happened that nobody ever meant to happen. By the time they pulled in front of the hotel and parked, Brody was already out and heading toward the lobby.

Nate raced to catch up. "We can't storm in and freak her out by coming on too strong."

"That depends on whether Bullard got hold of the hotel and whether the staff were willing to help or not. Sometimes we have some connections over here that are helpful. Other times it seems the opposite is true, you know?"

"Connections?" Nate repeated.

"Friends of ours." Brody shook his head. "We find having a lot of people we stay in touch with worldwide to be helpful when we run into chaos. A lot of our team has expanded to include other teams covered by other bosses, such as Bullard," he explained. "So, every once in a while, we need to use their services, and they need to use ours. So, in a sense, between us all, we have a vast network."

"Networks are good," Nate murmured, as he stepped into the hotel lobby, his gaze taking a hard left to a woman sitting in the farthest corner. Her knees were up against her chest, staring around the world, almost panicked. "She's at nine o'clock."

Brody turned and nodded. "That would be my guess too." The two of them slowly approached.

As soon as she saw them, her gaze darted from left to right, as if she were ready to run.

Nate held out a hand. "I'm Nate. I think you're expecting us."

She frowned at him and let out a broken laugh. "I was expecting you half an hour ago. The hotel didn't let me use the phone again, so I've been sitting here, wondering what I was supposed to do."

"What you're supposed to do," Nate replied, with a gentle smile, "is trust us. We're here now, and we'll help you get out of this."

She looked up at him, her gaze going from one to the other. "Are you sure? How do I know you're even who you say you are?"

Nate pulled out his ID and showed her. "See? I'm definitely who I said I am."

She snorted. "This could be completely fake."

"It could be." He studied her carefully, seeing the fatigue and the helplessness on her face. "But then the story you told Bullard could also be completely fake." Her eyes widened in outrage, and he smiled. "See? Being questioned doesn't make you feel very good."

"No, but having just escaped a kidnapping, if it keeps me safe, I really don't give a damn."

"Got it," he murmured. He walked over and sat down beside her. "Look. We're here because Bullard contacted a friend to say that you were in trouble. As I was told, you were on your way over to Africa to take a job with him, and you never made your Paris connection."

She slowly relaxed and nodded. "That's true." She shuddered, wrapping her arms tighter around her knees. "If you have questions about what happened, I don't really have a whole lot to tell you."

"And that's part of the problem. Were you drugged?"

She shrugged. "I don't know. The other woman kidnapped with me complained about a really bad headache, and it was probably because of the drugs that they gave her. I don't know if I was drugged or not." She took a deep breath. "My arm is sore, but I haven't checked it to see whether I can find an injection site or not."

"In that case I suggest we get some blood tests done, so

we can figure it out, then go from there."

She looked at him, unfocused, but she didn't move. "I don't want to go to the hospital."

He stared at her. "Do you want to stay here?"

"God no," she replied, bolting to her feet. "But I don't know where else to go, outside of you guys taking me to the embassy or something, so I can tell them what happened. Maybe I can get a new ID and passport there too. I just want to go home."

"What about the job in Africa?"

She shook her head. "I wasn't so sure I wanted to go in the first place, and, if this has shown me anything, ... it's that no way in hell I need to go over there," she cried out almost hysterically.

He winced, then reached out a hand to calm her. "It'll be fine."

She calmed a little bit and then nodded.

"Come on. Let's get you out of here."

Nate could tell that she wasn't so sure about trusting him. He hesitated, then did something he rarely would resort to. He opened up his energy and gave her a gentle, soothing hug. She almost melted into his arms, and he held her close.

When he eased up the energy, she stepped back and took a deep breath. "I don't know why, but I'm feeling a whole lot better now, so thanks for that."

He nodded formally. "You're welcome." He stared at her and watched closely as she gave Brody a tentative smile, then turned back to Nate and said, "Let's go." She stepped boldly toward the front entrance.

Brody asked Nate under his breath, "What the hell did you just do?"

Nate winced. "Something I almost never do and hated

to, but, in this case, I wasn't sure how to get her calm enough to go with us."

"It's a hell of a trick, man," Brody responded, his tone light but intense. "Not exactly sure what you did, so just wanted to confirm that it's all aboveboard."

"Always, always aboveboard." Nate shot him a hard look, his tone hard. "I don't do anything that's *not* aboveboard."

"Good, glad to hear that. Still that was a miraculous transformation in the trust department."

"It was," Nate agreed, with a smile. "And, not often, but every once in a while in the right circumstances, it's the perfect thing to do." As they caught up to Madeline at the front door, they each walked on opposite sides of her and led her to their vehicle.

Meanwhile Madeline nervously looked around at her surroundings.

"It's fine," Nate told her. "We'll keep an eye on you and for any bad guys." She didn't say anything but nodded. "Did they hurt you?"

"No," she whispered. "They didn't. We woke up in the hotel room, and we were talking, when an unmasked man came in, one of our captors, and he didn't seem to be very happy about our being there. He asked if we spoke French, which I don't, but Anna did. No other questions. When he went to leave, I asked him if we could use the bathroom. Since we were tied up, both our hands and our feet, we couldn't get there without help. So, he undid our bonds, still seemingly quite pissed off and upset about the whole thing. Soon he left."

Nate nodded at that. "Okay, that's good information."

"It's no information," she argued, frowning at him. "We

never saw him again. … Believe me that I'm grateful that we didn't see anybody else after that."

"How did you get out?"

She explained about the cleaning lady, asking her to use her keys to let herself in because they couldn't make it to the door. "We assumed we were locked in or at least guarded outside the door, since the unmasked man left us untied. But we had been tied up for so long that our feet wouldn't hold us up at first. Anyway, when the cleaning lady came in, we told her that we would step out so she could do her cleaning, and then both of us just … ran."

"So, chances are, your disapproving visitor wanted you guys to escape on your own," he noted, with a nod. "That's definitely a sign of remorse."

"Or it's a sign of a falling out among thieves," Madeline suggested, with a hard laugh. "I mean, no way one lone guy could have gotten the two of us into that room without some help, especially if we were both drugged at the time. And how do you carry two unconscious women into a hotel lobby and not draw attention?"

"Good points," Brody agreed. As they all got into the vehicle, Brody took over the driving and headed toward the hospital.

When they got there, Nate looked at her and said, "Come on. I'll go in with you."

She hesitated, then nodded. "Fine," she grumbled, "but I really hope they don't do a ton of testing."

He studied her. "Meaning?"

She shivered. "I guess a part of me doesn't really want to know what they might have done while I was unconscious."

He nodded with understanding. "And yet it's probably still better if we *do* know. It might very well confirm that you have nothing to worry about. Plus, there may not be a whole lot to understand. Maybe they drugged you long enough to put you in the hotel room, while they figured out what to do, then decided it was best to just walk."

Inside the hospital, he found they were expected, and that surprised Nate. Later he found out that Bullard had some pull here, and, once she was thoroughly checked over and released, Madeline smiled at Nate, almost in relief.

"You were right to find out for sure. I wasn't assaulted while I was out of it," she shared, "and it's much better to know that. I'm just exhausted and want to go home now. Is that … I don't know whether that's something you guys can arrange or not. If not, just help me get a phone. I'm not even sure what to do at this point," she admitted, wrapping her arms around her chest. "This is very much out of my wheelhouse, and, without an ID or any cash, I won't get very far."

He chuckled. "It's not usually in anybody's wheelhouse," he replied, with a smile. "Not many people get kidnapped or have the experience to know how to handle it."

She gave him a ghost of a smile. "I hear you. Yet somehow it feels very much as if I'm supposed to know what to do."

"There isn't any knowing what to do with a first-time victim," he noted. "Too much scarcity of information. If you'd gone to the consulate, they would have helped you, but we got to you first. So, now we'll go to the consulate and get your paperwork going because I don't think you'll get in or out of the country without it. Then we'll get you a phone and take it from there."

But when they got to the consulate, it was too late in the day to process a passport. She groaned, and they at least started the process, but she would have to come back the next day. Nate took her to an electronics store, where she got a phone that they paid for. It would take a few hours before her service actually began.

She hesitated when she accepted it and asked in a meek voice, "Who will I owe for all this? I was heading to Bullard for a reason, and it's called *a job*."

"Right," Nate replied. "I don't have a clue. For now, it's just on my expense account."

She snorted. "Nice to have one of those."

"It absolutely is," he agreed, with a smile. "Now, let's go get some food, and then we'll check into a hotel."

At the word *hotel*, she froze.

"A different hotel," Nate clarified gently. "We all need to get some rest for the night because tomorrow is likely to be more of the same."

"God, I hope it's not anything close to the same," she cried out.

"That's not my intention. We just need to confirm that we don't have any more trouble and that whatever is going on stops."

"Good."

AS THEY SAT in the car in the parking lot, setting up her phone for her, Brody's phone rang.

Terkel's tone was hard. "Where are you?"

He explained, and Terkel continued in a harsh tone. "Stay where you are. The police are on their way."

"What?" Brody asked, "Why?"

"I'LL EXPLAIN, BUT confirm she can't hear you." At that, Brody looked over at the other two and got up. "I'll just step out and take this." He exited the vehicle, leaving Nate to look at him with an eyebrow raised. He looked over at Madeline, but she was studying her phone, trying to remember key phone numbers.

Nate told her, "Not much chance of getting your other phone back, though it's hard to say for sure. Maybe it will be found in the hotel room or something."

She shrugged. "Maybe. I have a couple numbers in my head because I use them all the time, but, other than that, I don't remember much. I'll have fun trying to figure out other numbers."

He chuckled. "You'll probably find that one number will lead to more."

"I hope so," she agreed, "but then I guess people lose their phones all the time, don't they?"

"They sure do, and, as you know, we're on it."

She smiled at him. "Thank you. I really didn't have a clue about what to do, outside of calling Bullard or the cops, you know?"

"You did the right thing. Bullard then called my boss, who sent us to come over and find you."

"That just blows me away." She shook her head. "I told Anna that we were lucky to escape and that we should tell the authorities about what happened to us, but she didn't want anything to do with it. She didn't want to talk to the police or anybody. ... I didn't know what to say to her. She was so adamant and just wanted to run."

"Think about everything you've been through and how

you felt when you saw us. It's the way you handle the situation that makes all the difference," he pointed out. "I'm sure Anna felt she never wanted to dredge up any of this again."

"Maybe," she murmured. "I just hope she's okay."

"I do too."

Just then the car door opened, and Brody looked down at her. "Hey."

"What's up?" she asked.

"The police are on their way, and they need to talk to you."

She stared up at him, the color fading from her cheeks. "Why?"

"Outside of the fact that you were kidnapped," he began, with a smirk, "because they found a body in a hotel room."

"A body? In a hotel room?" she asked, staring up at him, shocked. "The same room I was in?"

He shook his head at that. "No, a different one."

She blinked. "And that has something to do with me, why?" she asked, staring at him in shock. "When will this nightmare ever end?"

"It will end," Brody declared in a smooth voice. "With any luck, it will be fairly quickly. However, at the moment, the police need to talk to you."

"Of course they do."

Just then two cruisers pulled into the parking lot, and Brody went to meet them. She grabbed Nate's hand. "Will you stay with me?" she asked, pleading and squeezing his fingers.

"Of course. We won't desert you. That's not happening."

She nodded but didn't look at all convinced.

When the first cop came over, Nate could see why she was scared because nothing but judgment and anger were in his expression when he spoke to them.

Nate knew this would be a disaster.

CHAPTER 4

MADELINE STARED UP at the cop, who seemed to think she was solely responsible for this blight in his day, and absolutely nothing she told him again for the third time now seemed to be anything he wanted to hear. After the first conversation in the parking lot, the police had insisted they head down to the station and give a formal statement, which she'd done, and thankfully Brody and Nate had stayed close by.

Only recently did Brody get up and leave, but Nate, true to his promise, had stuck with her. He'd also fielded as many of the questions as he could, giving them numbers to trace and people to contact, all regarding why and how they had gotten to her. Thankful that many of the Parisian police were bilingual and even multilingual.

When the same questions came around yet again, she yawned and shuddered. "I need to rest," she whispered, her voice fading.

The cop just glared at her, but Nate wasn't having anything to do with it. "That's enough," he declared, with finality. "Either charge her right now—though rest assured we'll be all over the media sharing how you treat your victims around here, without giving her a fair chance, even though she's answered every single one of your repetitive questions—or you let her leave now."

"You say she's a victim, but we don't have any proof that she's a victim. And neither is there any proof that there was ever this Anna person in there with you."

"Did you run a DNA sweep on the room?" she asked. "Short of that housekeeper cleaning up the doorknobs and things, the proof has to be there, and that can tell you all you need to know about Anna being there with me."

"The room was cleaned and cleaned thoroughly."

At that, she frowned and turned to Nate. "That's a little suspicious, isn't it? Have you ever known housekeeping to give a crap about things such as doorknobs?"

Nate studied her and slowly nodded. "A very valid point."

"What? So now you think the housekeeper is involved?" the cop asked in disgust.

"*Yes.* Since you're not charging me, I'm leaving." She stood and added, "It's clear you don't really want to hear anything I have to say, so you figure it out. One way or another, I'm about to collapse, and you can bet I'll have a heyday reporting your abysmal behavior once this is all over."

"Go ahead and report it," he replied, with an insolent tone. "We're trying to keep our citizens safe, and here you are making up stories and wasting our time."

At that, her fury boiled over. "Making up stories?" she cried out. "I was snatched from a bus in your city heading from the airport to downtown, where I'd booked a hotel for my layover. A tourist coming to your town, and you're blaming me for this?"

He just snorted, then got up and walked out, slamming the door behind him.

She sank down into the chair beside Nate. "What do

they want?" she cried out.

"Answers, but we have no idea why, but they seem so convinced you're involved."

"I don't either," she muttered. "So the dead man in a hotel room is disturbing in itself, but then they're thinking … I'm somehow connected?" She shook her head, feeling faint. "How does that make any sense?"

"It doesn't, unless they're not telling us something."

She stared at him. "I didn't do anything," she declared. "You've got to believe me."

He wrapped his arms around her in a warm hug. "I do believe you."

When her shudders eased some, exhausted tears filled her eyes. "I don't know what I would have done if Bullard hadn't sent you guys. I hate the fact that I'm coming apart at the seams," she muttered. "That's really not my style."

He chuckled. "When somebody hits the wall, their own style is revealed—whether they like it or not. We all have a breaking point. The fact is, you were also drugged, and the cops can check with the hospital to get those records too."

"But he doesn't want to."

Just then Nate's phone buzzed. He looked down and smiled. "That is the hospital right now. They just sent over the reports." He looked at it and whistled. "That should ease up some of the cop's panic. You were definitely drugged."

"Not likely with this cop," she muttered. "All it'll do is make them more suspicious of me."

"Maybe."

As the door opened, a different man entered this time.

Nate told him, "I just got the results from the doctor, so presumably you did too."

The newest cop nodded slowly. "It appears she was

drugged."

"Yeah, *ya think?*" she quipped bitterly. "Nice way to treat your tourists."

He winced at that. "We still haven't cleared you, but this goes a long way to making your story credible."

"I've told you the truth, whether you choose to believe it or not." She shook her head, shuddering again. "I'm about to drop, and I really don't want to go to the hospital again, nor do I want anything more to do with the Parisian police."

He nodded. "You can leave for now, but I need you to stay in town though."

She stared at him. "For real?"

He nodded. "Yes, for real, until we can get to the bottom of this." He handed them a card. "I'm Detective Manshue. I'll be conducting the investigation."

She looked over at Nate. "Do they have the right to make me do that?" she cried out, her voice quivering. She held up her hand, already shaking so badly that she wasn't even sure she could remain standing. Thankfully Nate was here helping her.

"Are you diabetic?" he asked sharply.

She shook her head. "No, but I do have blood sugar issues at times."

"Come on. Let's get you out of here."

The detective watched them go with a frown on his face.

When they got outside, Brody was there waiting, with their vehicle. He took one look at her, and concern filled his expression. "I've got a hotel for us nearby. We'll get some food right away. You don't look so good."

She nodded. "Food will help a lot," she whispered, sagging into the back seat and closing her eyes. When Nate's arms wrapped around her, she turned into them and whispered, "I just need a few minutes."

"Take as long as you need," he murmured against her ear. "You'll be fine."

"Maybe, … but it doesn't feel like it'll be fine." And her tears came then. "I'm sorry. I'm sorry," she sobbed. "I'm trying to hold it together."

"Don't bother," Nate replied, his voice gentle. "This happens after being drugged, and I'm surprised it didn't happen before this. You've held it together really well, but the gates have opened. You just need to let it pour out."

And, with that, it did.

NATE HELD MADELINE close and ushered her through the lobby area and straight up to the hotel suite that Brody had already arranged. When they got into the room, Nate led her to one of the bedrooms and pulled back the covers and just held her. Her sobs slowly relaxed, and soon he realized that she'd fallen asleep in his arms. Easing out from under her arms, he grabbed the blanket, covered her up, and tiptoed out of the room.

As he walked into the main room, he told Brody. "She's asleep. Whatever is going on has really hit her."

Brody nodded. "Do you find it interesting that they didn't ask her to ID the body?"

Nate frowned at that. "You're right. Why the hell not?"

"Maybe they just didn't get there yet, or maybe they're still trying to sort out who's good and who's bad in this whole deal."

Nate snorted at that. "They asked the same damn questions three times. I don't think they gave a crap. She seems to be a good suspect to target to close this case, and that's all that they were concerned about."

Brody nodded. "That's quite possible too. Unfortunately it happens."

"A little too often for my liking," Nate replied. "I would feel better if she was a hell of a long way from all this."

"I wish we'd gotten her out of here right away."

"Yeah, but the locals would have been after her anyway," Nate pointed out. "At least we have the hospital records, initial police reports, and the consulate visit to show that her story has been consistent all along."

"Yeah, you're right there. So, we'll have to see what we can come up with from here. Hopefully the police will be on it a little bit more now, instead of seeing her as their only suspect."

"I'm not sure they are there yet, based on the third degree they gave her," he muttered. He checked the time on his phone and asked, "Did you order food?"

"I did, but it'll still be a little bit though."

"That's fine. She'll need it when she wakes up. She'll also need clothes, unless we can we find her backpack."

"Did she leave it at the airport?"

Nate shook his head. "No. She didn't want to check any bags and had everything in her backpack. So my guess is that she carried it with her everywhere."

"Except we don't know for sure. We'll ask her about that when she wakes up. She might have checked it right through maybe, with her long layover."

"Yet it had her clothes in it, so she needed that bag. Plus, the airlines may not have accepted it for that long of a time period, especially for an international flight," Nate noted.

"It's probably with her purse and her passport," Brody

suggested.

"I didn't ask her if she had a purse," Nate grumbled.

"And that would have disappeared very quickly in a kidnapping case."

"And yet it could have been left in a dumpster near where she woke up too."

Brody pondered that and nodded. "You stay here and look after her, and I'll head over to the hotel and take a look to see if it was dumped or found anywhere."

"Also the police could have it and just haven't shared anything about that," Nate muttered. "I can't say that anybody at the Paris PD was too concerned about her welfare."

"Which really surprises me," Brody noted. "We have ego problems with MI6, but not everywhere."

"Maybe the locals got their feathers ruffled, since she didn't contact the police right away. Plus, we found her and took her to the embassy. Maybe it would have been a different story if she called the cops from the lobby on the hotel phone, but I'm not so sure about that. It seems to me that they're looking at her as being culpable or somehow involved in this case."

With that, Brody got up. "I'll go talk to them now. Then I'll see what else I can find when I search the area. Food will still be about an hour, and I should be back by then, If not, I shouldn't be too far off that timing." And, with that, Brody walked out.

Nate grabbed his laptop and sat down at the dining table to search for any news about the body found at the hotel. The fact that they hadn't asked Madeline to ID him already made Nate very suspicious. Maybe they didn't need her. Maybe they had pictures of her with him or something like that. "What would that entail?" he muttered, as he thought about it. "Hotel cameras maybe?"

As soon as he opened up telepathic communications with Terkel, he asked him, *Do we have any idea what's going on with her bags, her luggage, her purse, or anything? Do we have access to the hotel cameras?*

What would the hotel cameras tell you? Terkel asked.

The police never asked her to identify the dead body found in another room in that hotel or whether she recognized the man, he explained. *In fact, they view her as enemy number one. So I'm thinking maybe they saw something on the cameras, and, if that's true, I think we should know what it is too.*

I will have my team send you the feed. And, with that, he jumped out of Nate's mind.

Sure enough, Nate got an email about ten minutes later, and there was the feed. As he sat down and pulled it up, he watched as Madeline was walked in, obviously drunk. She had been drugged, after all, as confirmed by the hospital, so that was on point. She was with one man, assisting her greatly, but his hat was pulled down over his face. It was pretty-much impossible to see who he was. But, as Nate continued to watch the feed, a second man joined them, with no disguise at all. That was probably the dead guy in the morgue.

He contacted Terkel again. *Do we have a face for the man in the morgue?*

I do. Sending it now.

Sure enough, it matched. *So, the cops assume she knows him, even though it's obvious from the security feed that she's completely out of it.*

Yeah, I would say so, Terk agreed, *and that's disturbing in itself.*

Or they're just fishing and figured that this man had been a case of something gone wrong, even if she was a captive, or maybe the cops think she killed the man trying to escape.

Terkel confirmed. *That would be my assumption as well, but they're certainly not considering her a victim in this, and they should be.*

Yeah, I would have thought so, but you know as well as I do that just because we have one take on it doesn't mean law enforcement has the same.

Terkel snorted and ended the telepathic connection.

Nate was drained after that short telepathic exchange and would use the phone if needed later. Then he heard a sound and looked up to see Madeline at the bedroom door, staring at him, rubbing her eyes. "Hey, you need to come see this."

She stumbled over to him, sat down, and watched as he ran the feed again. "I was walking?" she cried out.

"Yeah, but obviously you were not in good shape. You can tell that you're drunk or drugged but completely out of it."

She nodded slowly as she stared at it. "Good God. What about Anna?"

"I didn't get any feeds with her," he said, "and that could be why the cops think you're lying when it comes to this other woman."

She stared at him. "Her name was Anna. She had shoulder-length brown hair, pinned atop her head. She had fine facial features, like a china doll. She was pretty and spoke French. I can't imagine why she wouldn't be on these feeds."

"It's possible she was brought in before or after you were," Nate guessed. "I'll go back to the earlier and later feeds." And that's exactly what they needed, but he didn't have access to it. "I'll ask Terkel to get it for us." He quickly sent him a text.

"What about the police?" she asked, staring at him. "Wouldn't they have automatically checked more of the feed?"

"I can't guarantee that," Nate muttered. "Unfortunately that would be a little more than the police are willing to tell us right now."

When her stomach grumbled, Madeline asked, "Can we get some food?"

"Brody ordered something from the hotel. It should be here shortly. How about a granola bar and some coffee in the meantime?" He stood to head into the kitchen.

She patted his back and shook her head. "I can get it."

Terkel sent him a link a few minutes later, and he opened up the feed. "We'll start with the next twenty-four hours." As they went through it, they saw another couple, and the woman had long black hair and wore a hat, when walking to a hotel room. When the man left the next morning, she didn't leave with him.

"You said she's a brunette with shoulder-length hair, right?"

Madeline nodded slowly. "Can you bring up that face for me?" As soon as he did, she cried out, "My God, it's her. It's Anna."

He stared at Madeline, then back at the video. "So, she's in a disguise?"

She nodded. "Yes. She has to be. That's not her hair. She didn't have long black hair. It was a shorter length and definitely brown."

"Yet she has black hair and a hat here, but what about the clothing?"

She shrugged. "Anna was in jeans and a T-shirt with me, not a dress. And she didn't have a purse or anything else, just like me."

"What are the chances that she spent the night with the first man, and then he left her as a prisoner?"

"And yet she told me that she spent the night with her boyfriend, then caught the bus and headed downtown to the café." She sat back, her mouth working for a moment, until the truth dawned on her. "She was in on it," she cried out. "Seriously, she was in on it?"

"Maybe. How about this second man? Do you recognize him? He joined up with you and your escort." Nate rewound the feed and stopped it abruptly.

"Oh my God. That's him. That's the unmasked man who visited us in the hotel room, right before we escaped." Madeline shook her head, frowning. "But Anna was terrified when she woke up. I woke up first, and she was lying there, tied up, just like I was. When Anna realized what had happened, she was absolutely panicked. And she didn't seem to recognize that man who came to our hotel room. I don't see how this is possible."

"That's fine," he replied, gently patting her hand. "Just because we don't know how it all fits together doesn't mean that it doesn't."

CHAPTER 5

MADELINE RUBBED AT her eyes yet again, as if trying to scrub away her recent memory of seeing Anna in disguise. "I can't see how or why," she repeated for about the tenth time, which didn't help. She was still completely flummoxed at the idea that this woman she had so briefly been incarcerated with may have been right in the middle of their kidnapping.

Nate added, "It's possible she had no idea that it would morph into this either."

Madeline grasped onto that suggestion with relief. "Of course not, and maybe, even if she did know part of it, she didn't really realize what it would entail."

He smiled at her. "You appear to be quite happy to let Anna off the hook."

She sighed. "It's not that I'm trying to let her off the hook, but honestly it's hard to see that she could have done this. But I don't know that for sure, do I?"

"No, you sure don't. Plus, it's way too early for any answers."

"Yet it shouldn't be," she declared, staring at him. "How hard could it be at this point?"

"Very hard. We have confirmed that the second man on the hotel cameras is the dead man in the morgue."

She shuddered and sank back onto the couch. "God,"

she whispered up at the ceiling. "I wonder if he had any idea that the last thing he did would get him killed?"

"I think the minute he objected to what was happening or why you were there was probably the last straw for whoever he was working with. I don't think he had any hand in you guys being kidnapped, and I don't think he had any intention of playing along. When the higher-ups decided to cut their losses, that meant getting rid of him."

She swallowed and nodded. "It still sucks," she muttered. "He didn't seem all that bad." She gave Nate a sad smile. "He was mad at whoever kidnapped me and Anna. Maybe because of him we escaped."

"Definitely the cleaning lady let you leave. Yet your visitor's fate was sealed because you escaped or maybe because of the kidnapping crew's own internal conflicts."

She winced at his wording. "Oh God, and for that I'm so sorry," she whispered. "He didn't seem to be a terrible person at all."

Nate grimaced at that. "If he had anything to do with the kidnapping, I wouldn't give him a pass quite so fast. There had to be a reason he was involved with the others, and you know what they say. You lie with dogs, you get up with fleas."

"You're right about that," she muttered. "I don't intend on giving him a pass. I just hope that Anna is okay."

He eyed her curiously.

She shrugged. "I don't know why I want to believe her so badly, but, when she was in that room with me, she was terrified. Whether she knew what was happening or what would happen to her, I don't know. All I can tell you is that she woke up beside me and was absolutely horrified to be in the position she was in. As soon as she could, she was gone."

"And now that leaves me wondering if she's really safe."

At that, Madeline stared at him in horror. "Why would the kidnappers go back after her?" she asked in shock. "Hasn't everybody been through enough already?"

"As far as you're concerned, the answer to that question is yes. However, as far as these bad guys are concerned? I'm not sure your feelings or inconvenience even come into play."

She shuddered, then looked around. "I need to get out of here. Like out of town. I need to get far away."

"I hear you, and that's a good idea, but we also have to deal with the police. You don't want to run because that will make you look guilty, and they will consider you a fugitive on the loose."

"I get that, but they're looking at me for kidnapping *and* murder, a murder of a man I didn't have anything to do with. They aren't looking at me as a kidnap victim at all, and that's what I am. And, if Anna is involved and is in danger, … for all I know, she'll throw me to the wolves too."

At her wording, he turned and stared.

She shrugged and added in a soft tone, "It's not out of the realm of possibility, is it? What's to stop her from going to the police and saying that I was involved, just to protect herself?"

"That would be an interesting twist," he agreed, with a nod. "Let's just hope that doesn't happen."

She snorted. "Yeah, I can hope all I want, but, so far, none of this has gone in my favor." She was breathing hard at this point. "I had nothing to do with any of this. I don't know any of the players involved, and, outside of waking up hog-tied in a hotel room, I don't remember very much. Not even how I got there."

"What about your travel bag?" he asked. "Did you have your bag or a purse? Did you leave it at the airport?"

She blinked, thought for a moment, then shook her head. "No, I only had a backpack, a good-size one. If the job worked out, and I stayed in Africa, I would go shopping for more appropriate clothing. I always travel light, and I didn't really think I would need very much."

"And you still may not need much. Finding your bag would help a lot though."

"That wouldn't have had anything to do with it, would it?"

He frowned at her. "Sorry?"

"A guy was homed in on my bag at the airport, when landing here," she shared, staring, yet not really looking at him, "and I felt weird about the attention he was giving it and me. I had just cleared customs and kept my bag really tight and close to me, as I headed outside. You always hear these terrible stories about someone stealing everything you have right at the airport, and he was making me uncomfortable."

"Interesting." Nate sat back and studied at her. "Did you get searched at customs or when departing?"

She shook her head. "No, not at all. It was pretty easy, just in and out."

He nodded. "And having done that, whatever was in your bag was free and clear. Then suddenly you get kidnapped, and your bag goes missing. That's interesting."

The color drained from her cheeks, as she stared at him. "So, it may have nothing to do with a conversation I heard on the bus?"

He shrugged. "It's possible those people on the bus were just conversing in an agitated state, but maybe somebody else slipped something into your bag to get it through customs."

"But that means he would have been on the plane and had already gotten it through customs once himself," she pointed out, "so that makes no sense."

"It does though. Did your bag get checked on the other side?"

Again she shook her head. "No, not searched. It went through the scanners and everything. I was all fine. Nothing got flagged."

He nodded. "But if they were carrying items that would have been flagged or had you transport items that might have been suspicious, it doesn't mean that you didn't get through okay. Did you look in your bag at any time? Did you see if anything was missing or different or suspicious about it?"

"No." She shook her head. "I had it with me the whole time. I got out of the airport pretty quickly, grabbed a bus to my hotel downtown, hoping to stop for coffee along the way. What a stupid decision that was."

"Maybe not," he countered, "because, if you hadn't, somebody could have decided it was easier to pop you in the airport. Maybe you wouldn't have made it back at all."

She blinked. "Seriously? Do you think Anna might have been a part of this?"

"I don't know what Anna's role in any of it was," he admitted, "but we can't rule it out."

"If she even had a role," she reminded him. "Let's not blame her for something she might be completely innocent of, since we really know nothing yet."

"Absolutely. I'm just trying to get some answers, and, as soon as we have more info, we'll know better where we stand."

When a knock came at the hotel room door, she let out

a stifled cry, slapping her hand over her mouth as she stared at him in terror.

He got up and called out, "Hello?"

"Room service," said the man on the other side of the door in a businesslike tone. "I have a food delivery for you."

He looked through the peephole on the door and nodded. Opening it, he studied the man carefully. "I'll just take the trolley."

The uniformed man hesitated, but, when Nate slipped him a large cash tip, the man made the cash disappear smoothly and nodded. "As you wish, sir." Then he turned around and quickly scurried down the hallway.

Nate brought in the trolley, shut the door, and smiled. "It's food."

She let out a shaky breath. "I'm glad, yet I'm not sure I can eat."

"You need to eat," he stated, his tone firm. "Absolutely no way we can have you continue with your nerves on edge like this all the time. Food will help calm you down."

She snorted. "I don't know what world you come from, but I don't think anything will help that."

He gave her the gentlest of smiles. "You're doing great, so don't give up now."

"No, I'm not doing great," she argued. "At this moment, it seems as if maybe I've been used as a mule to get something into the country. Then they kidnapped me to get my bag but let me go."

"I think I might know why they let you go."

She eyed him curiously. "Enlighten me."

He replied in a plain and simple tone. "If your bag contained whatever you were supposed to be carrying and if they got what they wanted, there was no need to kill you."

"No need to kill me?" She gasped, then closed her eyes. "That's a horrible way to put it," she murmured, her face in her hands.

"But it makes sense."

"In which case, why kill our visitor?"

"Because he could be identified, and he was in favor of letting you go. Whether or not that was part of the plan, who knows, but maybe he was disposable, or maybe people were pissed off at him, and that was a good way to handle a problematic member of their crime ring."

"I don't like the world you live in if these are the ideas that keep rolling through your head, especially with so much ease," she muttered.

"Yet you're a nurse, so you deal with all kinds of unpleasant things too."

"Yeah, but I deal with disease, sickness, and injuries."

"So, think of those smugglers who kidnap people as afflicted. Maybe their disease is a different kind, and their injuries are ones you cannot see, but surely you can understand that."

With a sigh, she sagged back into the couch and nodded. "Yes, in that case, that's quite true."

"I suggest we put it all to rest for the moment. We have food, and it's hot, so let's enjoy it."

She looked around curiously. "Aren't we waiting for Brody?"

"Nope, Brody knows the deal. He ordered the food, and he knew when it was coming. So at least we can enjoy a hot meal, even if he can't. He'll be here soon enough."

She looked at the food, then at him.

Nate added, "We really need this food, like it or not. It's fuel that we need, and food that is here for us, so we'll eat it now." And, with that, he opened up the trays and handed her a plate of roast beef, mashed potatoes, veggies, and some weird little puffy things on the side.

"I don't know what those are," she muttered, staring at them with doubt. "I've never seen them before."

"You're over on the French side of the channel," he noted, with a smile. "Maybe they do things differently here."

"Maybe," she muttered, but she walked over, accepted the plate, then took it back to the small dining table and sat down. "What if I can't eat?"

"You need to try," he answered firmly. "I don't know where we'll be or what'll happen next, but we need to be ready for anything."

At that, she frowned at him and asked, "Ready in what way?"

Such a wariness filled her tone that he burst out laughing.

"Ready to run?" she guessed.

"No, we can't leave the country. At least not with the cops on our tail. Unless they'll be complete assholes about this, then, in that case, yeah, we'll get you out of the country in a hurry."

She stared at him. "Really?"

"Yes, really. You didn't do it. I won't let you be thrust into a judicial process that could be completely screwed in this instance or taken over and twisted. Yet it's best if we deal with the cops upfront and legally, as long as we can."

"I agree with that," she muttered, as she stared down at the food. "I guess there's nothing to do but eat."

"Absolutely." And, with that, he sat down across from her with his own plate and dug in.

She smiled to see his obvious enjoyment.

He stopped, looked up at her, and chuckled. "There have been plenty of times when I've just been plain grateful to have food. At that point in time, it doesn't really matter if it's good or not, if it's hot or cold. It's food. It's fuel. We need it, so you better start eating." He pointed his fork at her.

She nodded. "Yes, boss."

And, with a smirk, she picked up a fork and got started.

NATE WATCHED AS she'd eaten. Then he managed to convince her to go lie down again. He wasn't exactly sure what drugs had been coursing through her system. He hadn't caught the names, though he probably should have, to see what he needed to be looking out for, but rest and food would have to do for now. With that thought in mind, he quickly texted Terkel, expecting a text in return.

Terkel phoned him instead. "How is she handling everything?"

"She's exhausted, stressed, and bothered too much. She finally ate, after I insisted, which is a good thing, and I've just convinced her to go lie down again," he murmured. "At this stage, she's paranoid."

"That's understandable."

"We did come up with another potential option as to what may have happened," he began, then explained about her travel bag that had gone missing and about the too-interested guy at the airport.

Terkel whistled. "That happens so often that it's amazing people even travel."

"That's because the average tourist doesn't know about

these shenanigans," Nate said, with a groan.

"If people knew that these guys were out there, trying to smuggle things through their bags, it would be a whole different story. In this case, it's quite possible that her bag is long gone, and chances are that their dealings with Madeline are all over."

"Unless they're afraid of her identifying them. However, considering they just killed one of their own men, I don't think that's really an issue."

"It might not be an issue," Terkel muttered, "but I'm not sure Madeline can safely walk away from all that just yet."

"The question is whether she's safe enough that we can escort her to Bullard's place? Or, if not that, what else did you have in mind?"

"Not sure. Let me think about this new information, and let's see what Brody comes up with." And, with that, he rang off.

Nate worked away at his laptop, writing up the little bit of information he had. Plus, he got the drug names from Terk that had been used on Madeline and hoped to do some research on what to expect. Suddenly he heard her cry out from the bedroom. Wincing, he knew she would have nightmares for a very long time.

He got up and peeped into the bedroom. She was curled up without any covers, shivering and crying out in her sleep. He grabbed a spare blanket, gently covered her up, careful to move slowly and surely, speaking in a soft tone, telling her it was okay and to take it easy and that everything would be fine. He also gently sent a blast of soothing energy to her.

She opened her eyes and looked up at him, and he saw her tears glistering in the half-lit room. "It'll never be okay, you know that," she muttered.

"But it will be," he argued, as he sat down on the side of the bed. "I know that sounds arrogant of me to say right now, but this will fade in time, and it won't seem to be such a horrific event in your life."

"That can happen anytime then," she muttered, "because, right now, I really don't want to deal with this."

He chuckled. "And with good reason. I know that this has been pretty tough on you, but you are safe here. So, once we can get you past all this police stuff, it'll get even better." She sniffled, trying to hold back the tears, and he added, "If you can sleep, it really would be the best thing for you."

"Yeah, and honestly I have been trying."

"You were asleep when I came in, but the nightmares are obviously overwhelming you a bit."

She hesitated. "I know this makes me sound like an idiot, but would you mind just sitting here, until I go back to sleep again?"

"Of course not. I was just working on my laptop anyway."

"Bring it in here then, and maybe I can go back to sleep."

And that's what he did. He sat down on the side of the bed, while she curled up beside him.

She was just about to drift off to sleep again when she whispered, "Do you think they'll find me?"

He looked over at her in surprise. "What makes you think they're looking for you?"

She opened her eyes and stared up at him. "Do you really think they'll just let me go?"

"If they are looking for mules to carry stuff through customs, borders, and crossings, they can't go around killing everybody. I think they ended up killing the one man who worked for them because he let you see his face."

She slowly nodded. "It's a sad day when somebody seeing your face gets you killed."

"It's a sad day when people use each other like this," Nate noted. "Yet it doesn't have to be *your* day, remember that."

She didn't say anything but shifted a little more comfortably into the bedding. "I really want to go back to England now."

"England, not Africa?"

She shook her head. "England," she repeated. "It'll be a long time before I travel again."

He could sympathize with her. She'd been through a lot already, but he wasn't sure how long it would take to get anybody out of here. "We have to get cleared by the police first."

"Right, and they're just looking for any scapegoat."

"I would hope not," he said, trying to make her think of other possibilities. "They need proof, not just suspicions."

"Proof," she cried out, in a strangled tone. "I didn't do anything, so there shouldn't be any proof. They don't seem to realize I'm a victim."

"I don't think they care. I know that sounds harsh, but that sounds about right."

"Yes, I know that because innocent people go to jail all the time," she cried out, "and I don't want to be one of them."

"Believe me that I'll make sure you aren't," he replied gently. "Just relax, get some sleep, and we'll talk when you wake up again."

She frowned at him. "You think I can just turn it off and

on?"

"You're a healer, for God's sake. Can't you just roll some of that energy down through your system?"

Her gaze widened, as she seemed shocked. "How do you know anything about that?"

"Because I work energy too." Nate grinned. "Not necessarily in the same way you do and definitely not in the way that Brody and his team does," he clarified, with an eye roll. She stared at him, and he just smiled. "But only in a good way."

"You say that," she muttered, "but I'm not exactly sure I believe it."

He just shrugged and returned to his laptop, but he didn't leave her bed yet. When he next checked on her a few moments later, she was breathing deeply, her chest rising and falling in a steady motion. He smiled and went back to writing up his notes on the case so far. None of it made a whole lot of sense, but he felt as if they were finally getting some answers. All he had to do was convince the police that she had nothing to do with this.

He smiled at that idea. He wasn't sure where he was heading from here, or what he was doing here either. However, if this was the kind of work that Terkel was asking him to consider, Nate wasn't against it. If people needed his help, he was always good for it. Plus, if it allowed him to use his abilities in a way that nobody else knew about, that was even better.

He certainly didn't feel bad about sharing his gift with her and making her trust him because, at the moment, she needed it. If she found out later that he had been keeping secrets from her, it might make her pretty upset, yet she had her own abilities and she should easily see the deception.

That was probably asking a lot of her in the state she was in, but maybe not. He wouldn't worry about it right now. He did what he needed to do for her at the time.

When he realized that she was sound asleep, he got up, grabbed his laptop, and headed out to the living room.

Brody walked in not very much later, carrying two coffees, and gave him one.

"How did you know she was sleeping and wouldn't want coffee too?" Nate asked.

He shot him a look. "Lots of ways, as you know."

Nate nodded. "I guess our gift makes life a little easier, doesn't it?"

"It does, but not always. Some people have walls we can't penetrate, and some people have abilities to do things that make us nervous," he pointed out. "But, as long as everything is done with good intentions, I don't have a problem with it."

"Meaning me, at the beginning of the op?"

At that, Brody nodded, looking dubiously at his now cold meal still on the cart. "Glad you brought that up. According to Terkel, you have abilities, but don't want to admit it."

Nate shrugged. "Not many people want to know that kind of information," he declared. "It makes you vulnerable, weak. In this world it's not easy on people like us."

"Oh, I agree, so thanks for the honesty."

"Right back at you," he muttered. "I don't have a problem helping Terkel, but I sure don't want it advertised that I have any paranormal abilities." Nate stared at Brody. "I'm surprised that you would."

"I don't want it advertised either, but I work within the confines of a safe group, and that makes a whole lot of difference."

"But can you trust the group?" he asked. "I mean, is it really safe? What if people still come after you because of it? Do you ever consider that?"

"We've had the best and the worst come after us already," he snapped. "I don't know if you heard all of what happened to our team, and I certainly won't fill you in on the major details, but let's just say that the government we worked for decided to terminate our team because we were too dangerous."

Staring at him in shock, Nate didn't even know what to say. "So, your employer tried to take out your team? How the hell is that even legal?" He spoke in a soft tone, careful not to wake Madeline.

"It wasn't legal, of course, but it was also the government," he stated. "They get away with an awful lot of stuff that they shouldn't do, much less get a pass. Believe me that we went to hell and back over it, but, in the end, we all survived, and we're all a lot stronger for it. Now we're private, independent, and don't have affiliations with any one government. If they want our services, they can pay for it," he shared bluntly. "And, so far, they appear to be quite happy to do so."

"And the US government? How did they handle it?"

"We haven't done any work for them. At the moment we've mostly been helping out the British government. Then, of course, we have a lot of private clients, and word of mouth is always much better where this kind of work is concerned. We have a lot of repeat customers too, and that works just fine for us."

"I can't imagine what you guys went through." Nate shook his head. "Or that you even continued to operate after something like that."

"If nothing else it made us more determined," he answered simply. "When you think about it, after you've been targeted in such a way, you know that you're much better off to stay together and to stay as part of a team you can trust, and that's exactly what we have. A team we trust, and that's why we're together in England."

"Why England of all places?" Nate asked. "You know it's wet and gloomy there."

Brody chuckled. "It is, but honestly, a lot can be said about having a safe place, where you can live peacefully and not be tormented by other people. We're set up in a well-fortified castle, although modern-day warfare could probably take it out in a heartbeat. With any luck, we'll have our own satellite one day and enough people on our team who are always aware, in case anybody else ever attacks us again."

"How many are on Terk's team?"

"Enough. And, with the previous department being neutralized, and no more attacks coming from them, that is the goal."

"I'm glad to hear that for you guys. That had to have been pretty rough."

"It was horrific, and all of us suffered in ways that you can't even imagine," he added. "It took weeks for many of us to come back online."

At his phraseology, Nate eyed him. "And you mean that exactly as you said it, don't you?"

He chuckled. "I sure do. The good news is that Terkel knew several healers, and he called them into play to try to save us. Some of the admins were killed outright, and, for that, we will always be incredibly angry at the job the government did on us, but, of course, being government and all, … it's not as if any of them will go to jail for it."

"No, of course not," Nate muttered, "but they should."

"Absolutely. The admins worked with us and were part of our team. Unfortunately they were taken out first. I don't know why, but I presume it's because the government thought most of us were down and already neutralized. Thus, it was up to them to take out the rest of the admins, so nobody could get back online again. But all it did was make us even more determined to get back on our feet, functioning at a level way higher than what they could even comprehend," he declared. "And that's where we are now." And, with that, he sat down with a plate. "I'll eat some of this and have my coffee, then go grab a few hours of sleep. I admit to being tired and frustrated after that worthless trek."

"Good," Nate replied, "sounds like a plan."

"Unless you want to sleep first, considering she'll be awake soon?"

"No." Nate motioned to the spare bedroom. "You go down first. You've been on the run just as long if not longer than I have. It'll do her good to see that we're relaxed enough to knock off for a while, you know? When she wakes up, I can sleep for a few hours. She's still pretty freaked out."

"Can't say as I blame her. That just makes her smart." He hesitated, as if not sure he should be asking, but he did anyway. "Have you picked up anything about her abilities?"

"No, though I did bring up energy work, when she told me that she couldn't sleep. So I told her, since she was a healer, she should just open up some of those energy channels and help herself. She seemed quite surprised that I knew anything about it, but that's for another discussion. She's still pretty upset over the one guy who died."

"She likely will be for a while."

"Have you talked to Terkel about our current theories?"

"Yeah, and taking the guy out does make some sense, no matter what started the whole thing. Letting himself be seen wasn't a smart move. Nobody wants anyone to be identified in these smuggling rings, and, if he was that casual about it and already pissed at whoever had put her there to begin with, he was probably marked right from the beginning. He didn't do his job, and he exposed them all to be captured, so they took him out." He shrugged. "He should have known better."

"I even wonder if they didn't let him know exactly what was going on intentionally and set him up."

"Not the first time that has happened," Brody noted, with a glance over at him. "If you think about it, that stuff happens quite regularly."

"As far as her abilities, she didn't volunteer much or anything really about what she could or couldn't do," he shared cautiously. "But then I don't think any of us do really, do you?" He looked over at Brody quizzically.

Brody shook his head, pushing aside the cold food with a grimace. "No, most of us keep pretty quiet about it," he admitted. "Terkel wasn't surprised when you wouldn't admit anything either way."

Nate nodded. "Yeah, I never really saw the reason to do that. I'm not into anything that sounds like bragging. Plus, aside from what I can do, I know little to nothing about this stuff anyway. Not to mention it can get a guy's ass kicked."

"Oh, good," Brody quipped cheerfully. "Sounds as if you'll fit right in." And, with that parting shot, he turned and headed to the second bedroom.

Nate had to admit he was wondering at his own willingness to consider a job with Terkel. Nate wanted to help others and doing it in a private way had worked well for Nate so far, but the jobs were a little far between sometimes. Plus, he had nobody to vet the jobs, which often became more of a problem. Additionally, as other people found out about his abilities, it would become a bigger problem every damn time to keep his secret.

Not exactly something he wanted to deal with, but, if Terkel's bunch gave him a backup partner, like Brody, then that made this change even more beneficial. Once again it was all conjecture, and Nate wasn't exactly sure that's what he wanted to do in life, but it was something to consider.

As he sat down, working on his laptop, he was now searching for pictures of Anna at the hotel's front entrance to see whether she had indeed left, or if something else had happened to her. He didn't want to bring that conjecture up to Madeline, in case it upset her, but definitely something was wrong about the whole scenario with this mystery woman named Anna.

If Nate could get some clarity on Anna's existence and her escape, that could really help Madeline's case with the local cops, even if Madeline didn't like what Nate had uncovered regarding Anna. Not to mention the fact that he needed the cops to back off on suspecting Madeline at every turn, so any proof he could get to help verify her story would make that interaction with the local authorities easier as well.

He wasn't having any luck at first and then *bam*. Eureka!

He cried out in triumph a few moments later, as he finally made it into the hotel's security cameras. They'd already been sent into archives to be deleted the very next day. He quickly raced through the video feed and froze when he saw the woman known as Anna, racing out the hotel's front doors.

"That's definitely her," he muttered, as he froze the frame and snapped a shot of it, then stored it away as he continued. But what surprised him was, as she got outside, instead of running madly, she ran to a nearby parked vehicle. She seemed to know that the vehicle would be there, waiting for her. That completely changed things.

It also implied that she had a way to contact somebody, or somebody had contacted her and had told her what to do and how to get out of there. Another very interesting change of circumstances.

He pondered that while he skipped through the rest of the security footage to see Madeline now talking to the front desk clerk, asking to borrow a phone, then talking to Bullard thereafter. Very normal and standard interactions.

He skipped back to the moment Anna had raced out through the lobby's doors, as she'd looked around wildly for a moment and then bolted toward a vehicle. As he brought up the vehicle and enlarged it on his screen, he noted two letters on the license plate. He quickly jotted that down and sent a text to Terkel, along with the screenshots he'd taken of the woman dashing toward it. In his text he added just a single word. **Accomplice?**

He got a thumbs-up reply, saying the team would look into it.

And Nate knew they would. This wasn't a case of *when they got around to it*. This was a priority. He didn't know how many other cases Terk's team had ongoing at any given time, but, from a totally personal prospective, Nate had heard from Brody that quite a load of pregnancies were happening. That disturbed Nate somewhat because he hadn't spent much time around kids, although they seemed to like him just fine. He just couldn't imagine running a business and having to deal with being a new father too.

Yet, according to Brody, everybody seemed more than happy to be over there. Nate just wondered whether it was a long-term solution or a flash in the pan for the moment. He certainly knew of other companies that operated successfully in both the professional world and in the private world of living together—companies that almost everybody in this industry and the military knew about. For one, he knew about Levi and Ice, who had their place in Texas. Nate had often wondered at the ability of that family unit to pull it off. And yet it appeared that they were doing just fine too. So maybe Nate just hadn't found a reason to make it work for him on a solo basis because that's really what it came down to. You make things work when you need and want to. Otherwise you lingered on the sidelines, wondering how everybody else made it work.

He almost blanched at the idea of intermingling his work life with his personal life because it had been a very long time since he'd had a serious relationship that even made him want to consider the future. His gaze drifted over to the bedroom Madeline was in. There was something between them. Of course the fact that he'd used some of his energy to help calm her down and to make it a little easier on her was another mitigating factor, as the energy stayed in play until one or the other cut it loose. He knew he needed to disconnect, but it was easier to help her if he didn't sever that tie just yet.

When his phone rang, he looked down at it and frowned. "Hello?" he asked cautiously.

"I'm Detective Manshue from the Paris Police Department," announced the man on the other end. "We want to speak to you both as soon as possible."

"Madeline is sleeping right now." Nate glanced toward the bedroom, frowning. "What can I do for you?"

There was a moment of hesitation on the other end. "We need her to ID a body."

"You mean that the man who came into the room where she was being held captive?"

"A different body," he answered, his voice almost apologetic.

"A different body?" Nate repeated, his heart sinking because he knew what was coming. There was no way *not* to know, yet he really hoped it wouldn't go that way.

"Yes, a female body."

"Damn. I guess you're thinking it's Anna, the woman Madeline was kidnapped with."

"Possibly. We've checked the hotel cameras, and she ran out the front entrance but appears to have gotten into a vehicle on her own."

"Right," he muttered, not letting them know he'd already seen the same video. "What happened then?"

"We don't know," the detective admitted. "However, her body was found in a dumpster not very long ago. We're just not sure whether it's the same woman or not."

"Of course," he said, swearing softly in his head. "I'll talk to Madeline as soon as she wakes up, and, no, I won't wake her. She's exhausted, stressed, and worn out from the treatment she's received in this city, both from the police and the kidnappers," Nate explained. "As soon as she's awake, I'll call you back and let you know when to expect us." And, with that, he rang off, then sat here, staring.

When Terkel contacted him by phone a few minutes later, he asked, "Did the police call you?"

"Yes," he confirmed, then quickly filled him in.

"Damn," Terkel murmured. "I was really hoping it wouldn't go in that direction."

"You and me both," Nate agreed. "This will be hard on Madeline when she wakes up, but at least she's getting some quality sleep."

"This will definitely be hard, but some of these answers have to come out, and the sooner, the better."

"Oh, I agree with you. The fact that Madeline has to ID Anna will just make it that much worse."

"She's stronger than she looks," Terkel noted. "And I get the whole protectiveness thing, but there are limits to what we can do along those lines."

Nate winced. "Is it that obvious?"

"Oh, yeah." Terkel laughed. "It's very obvious, but there are limits to what we can do. So, in this case, you need to see if she can ID the body, and then we'll go from there."

CHAPTER 6

MADELINE WOKE UP and remained in bed for a moment, letting all the scary and the good memories filter back in again. The fact that she was no longer a captive was incredibly enlivening. She slowly sat up, looked around, and realized she was alone in the bedroom. Then, hoping that she wasn't truly alone in this hotel room, she stepped out to the living room to see Nate working furiously on the laptop.

He looked up, put aside his laptop, and walked over to her. "How do you feel?" he asked, reaching out for her shoulders.

She went into his arms and just let him hold her, wondering at the need for that. She'd never been much of a hugger before, and yet, with him, it just seemed natural somehow and easy.

He stepped back so he could assess her features. "Are you doing okay?"

"I'm hungry."

"We figured as much. We have some sandwiches and prepared salads, so we could always offer you something."

She smiled. "Thanks."

"You look much better."

She gave him a goofy smile. "How would you know if I look better?" she asked, with a chuckle. "You've only ever seen me at my wit's end."

"Compared to that at least," he clarified, "you look much better."

She smiled. "You're just trying to be nice."

"Yeah, that's me," he quipped. "I'm always trying to be nice."

"You are. Even when I'm not being nice, you are still nice," she offered, with a smile. "It's a sobering realization that other people are accustomed to dealing with these scenarios. They are so horrific for those of us caught up in them that we can't even imagine what it would be like to deal with more than one of these kidnappings."

"Isn't that a good thing? And other people like us are around. Stop being so hard on yourself. Life is still good in many ways, so be thankful for that."

"I won't argue with that," she murmured. "I'm just grateful that I've come this far and that I'm safe." She looked around and smiled. "What are the chances of getting coffee? I would also really love a shower too."

"All of the above are possible," he replied, then took a deep breath. "Meanwhile, the police just called a few minutes ago."

Her stomach knotted, and she stared up at him, fear taking over her common sense. "What did they want?" she whispered.

"They want you to identify a body."

Her eyes widened, then her stomach clenched even tighter. "The man they found at the hotel?"

"No, somebody else." Then he took another slow, deep breath. "A woman."

She cried out, her hand going into a fist, then straight to her mouth, as she stared at him in shock. "Oh please, no," she whispered.

"I'm afraid so. They believe it's Anna."

She shook her head frantically. "But that would mean they got rid of her too."

"Which is not beyond the realm of possibility," he reminded her. "Whether she was part of it, caught up in it, trying to escape it, or some combination of the above, all are possible, but we have no idea at the moment. We can't judge her too harshly, and, if she is in the morgue, that's even more reason to figure out what the hell is going on."

"When did she die is the next question," she pointed out. "I hate to even say it, but will that clear me?"

"It's possible," he acknowledged. "I mean, it's definitely possible, but I won't hold out any hope, not until we confirm it's her. Hopefully the cops have some cause of death, time of death, and anything else that might help us prove your innocence."

She curled up on the couch, pulled her knees to her chest, and stared at him. "I need coffee and a shower and a change of clothes before we go," she whispered, "and, for the record, I really don't want to go at all."

"But don't you want to know for sure if it's her?"

She gave him a haunted look. "Yes, of course, but really I would prefer to know that she's okay. But, if it's her, it's the worst news." She was shivering now. "I was hoping this would all just go away."

"It won't go away until we get to the bottom of it," Nate stated, "and this appears to be what we need to do to make that happen."

"That next part is really horrific," she murmured. "When you think about it, how many other people can turn up dead?"

"If Anna and the one guy who you saw are both in the morgue, then it's two people who had a connection to you that you could identify. Still, I don't understand why they would take out Anna."

"Maybe they were supposed to take her out in the first place," Madeline suggested. "I just can't make sense of any of this."

"Which is why we'll go down to the station, and we'll do the identification, and we'll leave it there."

She stared at him. "How does one leave it there?"

He smiled. "We'll work on it together, but obviously we need to ID her. So let's get you in for a shower, and you'll feel better." He studied her, trying to keep her calm with his words, yet he could see the panic coming off her in waves. "If you want, I can go down to the hotel lobby. A gift store is there, and maybe I can find something for you to wear."

She stared at him. "From the gift shop?" she asked, her voice rising.

He shrugged. "If you prefer, a couple department stores are not too far from here. I can go get you something to wear to the police station."

"Does that mean you *don't* want me to go shopping?" she asked cautiously.

"I would just as soon you weren't seen in public. I don't mean that to scare you. I just want to keep you safe. Now that we have Brody back—he's lying down and is due to wake up in another half hour or so—why don't we order some coffee and a hot meal too? When he's up, I'll go get you some clothes. It won't be fancy, just some essentials."

She waved her hands. "I don't wear fancy anyway. Leggings and T-shirts would be just fine," she said, taking a deep, calming breath. "And coffee. Coffee would be good. I need to clear my head. This isn't how I had hoped to wake up."

"Of course not. But you did wake up, and it's good news for you in that at least Anna's been found, not in ideal circumstances, obviously. However, with any luck, we can get a time of death for her. Once the cops connect the facts that the dead man and Anna were in that hotel together, maybe that will release you from being one of their suspects. Not to mention Anna left in a car."

With that agreement in place, he ordered coffee and then phoned the police and made arrangements to get Madeline into the morgue to see the body in two hours, with proper precautions. Once the coffee was delivered, he woke up Brody and then told her, "I'll head out now. Be back as soon as I can."

MADELINE NODDED TO Nate, who quickly left. With Brody sitting beside her, sipping coffee, she frowned at him.

Brody raised an eyebrow. "He'll be fine, you know?"

She shrugged. "I guess I shouldn't worry about him, since he appears to be much better at handling all this than I am. Yet, I am worried."

"Don't be. He has experience with any and all things. Rarely do victims in kidnappings have experience to draw on."

"You would think that they wouldn't want to either," she muttered. "The fact that it even happened in the first place is crazy, so I can't imagine it happening a second time."

"It does, unfortunately," he pointed out. "So, we're trying to avoid any of that happening in your case."

"I don't understand why they would have killed Anna," she muttered, looking at him directly. "It makes no sense to me. If she was already free and clear, why kill her then?"

"More to the point, why was she in there in the first place? If we can figure that out, then we'll have a good understanding of what went wrong in her world."

"You think somebody betrayed her, don't you?"

"The options aren't great." He took his empty coffee cup and walked over to the coffee service and poured another cup. "Do you … want some?"

She smiled and nodded, amused that he was uncomfortable being nice to her.

Brody shook his head, brought over their coffees, and continued. "Why would Anna have gotten into that vehicle, unless she knew who it was? And why did she order a ride that you didn't know about and that she wasn't sharing with you?"

"I didn't even consider all that."

"The police are already running down the license plate of her getaway car. It's possible that she ordered an Uber or something similar that runs here. After that, maybe somebody else followed her or she met somebody else, and that person betrayed her. We don't know that the driver of the car itself has anything to do with it, and we won't know until we get more information," he shared.

"And that, of course, is the problem. I hate waiting for answers," she muttered, as she sagged back against the couch.

"Maybe, yet waiting for answers is sometimes all we ever have going for the investigation. When we get them, we must confirm that they are correct answers, you know? The fact that they've found this woman already means that she was left in a fairly public place. So, her killers wanted her found. Whether that was meant as a threat to you or was just carelessness on their part or maybe they didn't have the time, I don't know."

"None of this makes sense, so I don't understand what they could possibly want me for."

"I don't know either," he admitted, "but you were heading to Africa, and we do know that Bullard has enemies—and big enemies at that—so we're also wondering if it could be connected to one of his cases."

She blinked at that. "Meaning that they thought they could take me out as a warning to him or something?"

He nodded. "That's a possibility, yes. But again we're looking at all options. That sounds terrible I'm sure, but we don't really have much choice at the moment."

"Nate did find Anna leaving the hotel, per its own security cams. She was seen racing out, and the police have that video too. So in theory, shouldn't that prove my story is true?"

"In theory, yes," Brody agreed, "but there are other reasons why they might want to keep you on their suspect list. What we have to figure out is why."

She sighed at that. "They are playing games," she muttered. "Except I don't know the rules. I don't know how to play the game, and somebody else is pulling all the strings."

"They are," he agreed. "Absolutely they are. Until we get to the bottom of it, we won't have any idea what the game even is. When you woke up in that hotel room, did you have any possessions with you at all?"

She shook her head. "No, I'm still wearing the clothes I woke up in, and I don't have any of my belongings. I don't have my backpack, my cell phone, and my pockets are empty. I don't have anything."

He nodded. "What are the chances that the kidnappers think you are hiding something?"

"What could I possibly be hiding? They took everything," she exclaimed.

"The kidnappers seemed to be after something. What about Anna, the woman who you were with, did she have anything with her?"

Madeline thought about that for a long moment. "Not that I saw. Once the man untied us and let us go to the bathroom, I saw more of the hotel room than I had seen so far. Other than that, I didn't really talk to Anna much, as she slept a lot, and then we escaped. We both sat on the bed, but there wasn't a whole lot to say. She wasn't that friendly, and she was very scared," Madeline added, taking stock of her memories. "There was no way to hide that she was terrified."

"I think that's likely because she didn't expect to be on that end of things."

"Meaning, not a captive?"

"Exactly. I don't think she thought she would end up being a captive at all." He got up and paced the room. "So, it had to have been pretty sobering for her to realize that she ended up with you. So her escape would have been even more heartfelt and likely would have kept her away from anybody she knew."

"So, why jump in that vehicle then, with some stranger? Who did she leave with?"

He shrugged. "That's what we're trying to find out." Just then his phone rang, and he answered it. "Hello, Terkel. I'm putting you on speaker, and Madeline is here. Have you've got anything for us?"

"Yes, we were just discussing the vehicle that Anna escaped in."

"So, it was an Uber or something?"

"Looks like it."

"Okay, so what then? Was it just sitting there? Any sign of the driver?"

"Yes," Terkel replied, his tone hard. "We've located the driver. He was taken to the hospital and was pronounced dead upon arrival."

"What the hell?" Brody stared at her. "Why on earth would it be that important to take out Anna *and* the innocent driver?"

"The only reason that I can think of," Terkel replied in a sobering tone, "is if her driver saw what happened to Anna. If so, maybe the kidnappers are just mopping up witnesses."

"But this is, … I hate to say it, but this is one hell of a messy operation then, and that doesn't feel right. The kidnappers seemed to be smooth operators, until something blew up."

"Exactly. Something blew up, and that's the problem," Terkel confirmed. "Until we know what that is, answers are a little thin on the ground. All we're getting is way more questions." On that note, Terk ended the call.

"It doesn't make any sense," Madeline muttered. "Why kill an Uber driver for picking up a ride?"

"Because nobody wanted him to identify his passenger. The kidnappers had to cut their losses, so now Anna's dead. Maybe they killed her in front of the driver. Maybe they had to take out both of them at the same time to confirm nothing could be traced back to them."

"But what could she, … what could she possibly have known that would necessitate her being disposed of?"

Brody tilted his head. "What if she betrayed the kidnappers? What if she was involved, but then betrayed them, got loose, and somehow ended up in this situation?"

Madeline let out a heavy breath. "God, I just want to go home."

"We'll get you there," he murmured. "I heard you don't want to go work with Bullard?"

She nodded. "I just want to go home. And trust me when I say that I won't be doing any foreign travel for a very long time," she muttered. "If ever. I'll have to learn to live with this nightmare somehow. I was traveling to start a new job."

"And, if you had made it there, Bullard would have been an excellent employer," Brody shared.

She frowned at him. "You know Bullard too?"

"Yes, Bullard is somebody I've worked with for a while. He's been to our place in England several times as well."

She nodded. "That's good to hear. At least my initial instincts on that were sound."

"I don't think you can blame your instincts for whatever happened here. You have to trust strangers in this world, and sometimes things happen for a reason that we don't fully understand."

"Getting kidnapped and all this mess? Yeah, you're right. I don't understand that and don't think I ever will."

He chuckled. "No, and I'm sure anybody in your situation would say exactly the same thing. But remember that something is going on here that none of us really understands. So, until we can put that into play, that's just the way it is."

"*Great*," she muttered, sagging back. "I need a shower, and Nate is supposed to be getting me some clothes, but I also need food."

"So, no to the cold sandwiches, but you want a hot

meal? I'll order the food right now. With any luck, by the time you're done eating, Nate will be back with some clothes. Then you can have a shower, and we'll head to the morgue and identify Anna, if it's even her."

Madeline shuddered. "God, I was only with the woman for how long? Overnight?" She turned to Brody to get confirmation from him.

He shook his head. "Two nights, it seems because you never reached your hotel for the layover."

"Oh my God. We were both drugged the whole time, so I didn't even know for sure. When we escaped, I wanted her to stay close to me and to wait in the hotel, but she just bolted."

"Of course, because she already knew what was going on. She just may not have known who all was involved, and, chances were, whoever was involved is the one who betrayed her."

"So, a lover possibly," she whispered.

He nodded. "Often it is. People tend to trust until things go wrong, and it often turns out to be a betrayal from within. And sadly, most of time, we don't see it coming."

"Which really sucks." She curled her knees up against her chest and stared at him. "How do you ever trust somebody after that?"

"In Anna's case, she won't get that opportunity. In your case, you'll need to use your energy a little bit more to keep yourself safe."

She blinked, then eyed him carefully, contemplating his remark.

He laughed. "I work with energy all the time. I can see that you do too."

"I've always just used it for healing," she said. "I don't do very much with it. I just put healing energy out there."

"Next time you need to put up barriers, or at least a guard system, so when people don't have your best interests at heart, you'll recognize that you're in danger. It's simply a matter of putting energy out there, then assessing what comes back to you."

"I did that," she admitted. "Something was odd about the airport, and I didn't get coffee there but left more or less because I was scared. I don't know what would have happened if I had stayed at the airport."

"If you felt that way, then it's highly likely it could have been worse there. So don't judge yourself for getting yourself out of the airport. If these guys needed your travel bag, they would have taken it, one way or another," he noted, trying to make her feel better. "You didn't do anything wrong."

"Yet it feels as if I did," she muttered. When a knock on the hotel room door came a few minutes later, she asked, "How come your room service came so much faster than last night?"

"Because last night we timed it to be delivered later. In this case, you're hungry, and I'm hungry, and we need to eat." He got up, checked who it was before wheeling in the trolley of food. "Let's eat."

She hesitated. "What about Nate?"

"Nate will eat when he gets in. Don't worry about it. Besides, he should be back any minute."

She frowned but got up reluctantly to get a plate of food. "Nate doesn't send you messages to let you know it's all good or to check in on a regular basis?" she asked curiously.

"No. Generally, if I hear from him, it'll be to report a problem, or he needs answers, or something's held him up. If all is good, we don't worry about checking in."

She nodded. "That's good to know because I've been getting a really weird feeling about it."

He froze, then turned to face her. "A weird feeling? In what way?"

She stared at him. "It just feels wrong."

"Wrong in what way? Tell me exactly what you're feeling."

"It's hard to explain," she began. "I feel … as if he and I share a connection, and right now that connection is stretched thin."

"Interesting phraseology. Can you close your eyes and reach out to him mentally?"

"What good would that do?" she asked.

"All of us on Terkel's team can talk to each other telepathically," he shared. "It would be easier if we could all communicate that way. Then we could check in on a regular basis. However, he's new to the team, and we haven't got that system in place with him yet, but it's important right now."

"Telepathically?" she repeated, stuck on that.

He chuckled, then his tone turned urgent. "Yes, but listen. If ever you get a weird feeling, then tell me immediately. Now talk to Nate, if you can."

"How?" she asked.

"Just close your eyes, picture him in your mind, reach out mentally, and ask him if all is well."

She obediently closed her eyes and sent out a message, wrapping it up in a gold healing light, asking Nate if all was well. When her body jerked back with an answer, she opened her eyes in shock. "He said, yes."

Brody laughed. "That's good. So, I gather you weren't expecting to get an answer?"

"How does anybody expect to get an answer like that?" she asked in a hushed whisper, staring at him in awe. "What if that was my imagination?"

He lifted one eyebrow. "Was it?"

"I don't know," she wailed, raising both hands. "How am I supposed to know? What if I just made it up?"

He smiled. "Maybe you did, but considering the connection between the two of you, I would say it's not likely."

"Where did that connection come from though? I've never really met anybody I've felt that connected to, especially so quickly."

"For one thing it's the circumstances," he replied cautiously. "The other could be the fact that he's been using energy to help you deal with all this, to help you heal, and to help you sleep."

She nodded. "I knew he was, in a sense," she shared, "because I was really struggling, but I wasn't expecting a deeper connection to be forged by that."

Brody didn't say anything about that but motioned at her food. "Since Nate told you that he's fine, let's go with that, but let's eat just in case something does blow up, and we have to leave in a hurry."

She sighed as she stared down at the food. "I do get the feeling that you guys are used to giving orders a lot."

"We are, but, more than that, we're used to having them obeyed because it may save your life one day." She glared at him, and he just smiled. "Remember that we're doing this for a reason."

Her shoulders sagged, and she nodded. "Right. I do need to remember that, don't I?"

"Yes, you do, and right now you need to remember that we're all here for you, and it's not simply a case of getting you out of a hard spot. We need to confirm that this is over with. And, if somebody is killing people, we have to confirm you're not on the hit list."

She winced at that. "That is not a nice concept to think of."

"No, it sure isn't, and you're still not eating."

And, with that, she picked up the burger in front of her and started munching.

NATE WAS TAKING the long route back to the hotel, when Terk updated him on Garret.

"Seems the fates are working against us. Bullard's man Garret got delayed with mechanical issues on one flight and with a bomb threat on the next. He hasn't even left Africa yet. Now he's being detained because of some MI6 flag. We've got Jonas working on clearing that up."

Nate shook his head. "No worries. We'll see him when we see him. Meanwhile, Brody and I are handling things."

Nate ended the call, not wanting to expose his position. He felt someone behind him moving in his direction, so he wound his way into an alley and waited in the shadows of a dumpster. He didn't know what the hell was going on, but he felt as if he'd been watched from the time he'd left the hotel. He just wasn't sure who it was or why. As soon as the energy moved past him, he stood and called out to the plainclothes detective he'd met earlier, who was now in front of him. "Why are you following me, Manshue?"

The detective stilled, then turned and glared at him. "Because we don't know who you are and what you're doing here."

"Now that's bullshit," he spat. "You might want to know where Madeline is, but that's a whole different story, and there was no reason to not just call me and check in, as most people do."

"We don't know what you're up to right now, and, for all we know, you're all part of the bigger conspiracy. We have three bodies, and you've not been vetted."

"As it turns out, I'm very well vetted, if you would just check in with Terkel." He shifted his hands in his pockets and stared at the cop in front of him.

"Who thinks we want to deal with Terkel?"

"You may not want to, but it would be foolish if you don't." He gave him a smirk. "He's one of the most straight-up guys there is."

"Yet, my superiors tell me that he had some problem with the American government and that the US has cut ties with him."

"Sure, bound to be some fallout, considering they tried to kill him and his entire team." Manshue's eyebrows shot up, and Nate nodded. "Yes, that's what happened and he and his team have since gone private. However, if you want to make it an issue, feel free."

The detective studied him for a long moment. "Why did they try to take them out?"

"Because the government decided his team knew too much—you know, typical government bullshit."

"Everybody is okay?" he asked cautiously.

"Part of the admin staff was killed, but the team is back up."

"You were one of them?" he asked.

"Not at that time, but my partner was, and I can tell you right now that we don't take kindly to having people up in our business or following us around. Do yourself a favor. If you want to know something, just ask."

"Hey, I'm just following orders."

"You better confirm those orders are real orders and not just suspicions on your part," Nate declared, his tone equally hard as he stared down Manshue. "Because we have our own ways of checking up on people, and, for all I know, you are part of this kidnapping ring."

The detective's eyebrows shot up. "Good God, do you have any idea how prevalent the crime is in Paris?"

"Oh, I have a good idea. You've got a ton of prostitution, human trafficking, drugs, and everything else. It's really no different than every other major city in the world. But you're wasting your resources on me, when we already arranged to come down to the morgue to identify the woman you found. So what's the point of following me around?"

The detective hesitated. "I wasn't supposed to let you see me, so obviously I'll be in trouble."

He shrugged. "That's too bad, isn't it? What I want to know is what the hell they're doing chasing down Terkel's team because, if that's something you guys think will go unnoticed, you're wrong."

The detective shifted uncomfortably. "Look. We didn't have any way to confirm who you are. Especially since we knew you weren't part of Terkel's original team."

"Nope, I'm not, but Terk's team continues to grow. It's much bigger now."

"I can't imagine there are many people like you."

"You don't know anything about us, and don't even think about listening to all that useless gossip," he muttered.

"Yeah, well, that's what I told my bosses, but they

thought that maybe there was something to it."

"Ridiculous lies," Nate said, with a shrug. "Nothing special about the team except that the government tried to wipe it out and uses bullshit to muddy the water."

"Even that is suspicious though," Manshue pointed out. "You have to admit that most governments don't do that."

At that, Nate gave a hard laugh. "You're kidding me, right? That's what *all* governments specialize in. They make people disappear, and nobody ever knows. Nobody is ever there to question. You know that, so don't be foolish. You can just as easily take a walk one day, thinking you're heading off on a job, then turn around and find out one of your own team members is right there to pop you one. So don't give me that BS. The difference in Terk's case is that the government failed and got caught."

"I work with the police, not for one of these underground government organizations," Manshue clarified, "so that's not likely to happen to me."

Nate gave him a flat stare. "Do you really think that anybody who hasn't been somebody at the top of the pecking order hasn't been put in that same position before?"

The detective shrugged. "Maybe, … but that's not the world I work in."

"And yet here you are, following me, an ally who's here to cooperate."

"Yeah, and we don't know for sure you are who you say you are."

"Really? So, what is it you want from me for ID because you didn't even ask me for anything more than what we've already given you. Therefore, I'm calling BS on that too."

The detective flushed, then glared. "I just don't know what the connection is between the two of you."

"You keep adding all these extra little reasons why you're following me, but it's all still BS. I went to get some clothing for her because she ended up with only the clothes on her back after the kidnapping, the kidnapping you guys have completely ignored. You wanted us down at the morgue, so she'll get a shower and clean clothes and some coffee and food, before we head down there. I'm bringing the clothes back right now, so do you want to come up with me?"

"I …"

"I suggest you do," Nate said, cutting him off, and, with that, he motioned at the detective to walk beside him. When Manshue hesitated, Nate loudly declared, "I'm calling your bluff, Detective. You either come along and confirm this is what you were doing or it's not. Then I will put Terkel on your case to see just what the hell you guys are up to."

"We're not up to anything," he protested. "I could just feel something different."

"Different?"

"Yeah, between you and her," he muttered, with a shrug. "I don't know. I just get a weird buzz off the two of you."

"A weird buzz off us? That weird buzz is likely because we've grown quite fond of each other," Nate shared, tossing his head to the side. "But if that's *weird* for you, I'm not sure what else to say."

The detective flushed again. "Look. My instincts tell me that more is going on than it appears."

"There absolutely is more to this, and I was hoping you would find it. One of the men assigned to guard the kidnapped women is dead and in the morgue and was captured on the hotel's security cameras. Then the other woman, Anna, seems to have turned up dead. Anna, who was kidnapped with Madeline, and afterward they both escaped.

I understand you found the driver of Anna's getaway car, who was also found dead. So, what possible reason could there be for taking these three people out?"

"That's what I was trying to figure out," the detective said, as he fell into step beside him. "It makes no sense."

"It does if you think in terms of Madeline being forced to bring something through customs that she didn't realize she was carrying at the time."

"Or maybe she did know, and she's been a part of all of it the whole time."

"Ah, so you think she might lead you to some of the smuggling ring?"

"It's a huge issue here," he stated, his tone hard as he glared at Nate. "Anybody who can shed light on it is helpful."

"Sure, but not at the cost of Madeline's losing her life. As far as we're concerned, Anna was probably involved in the smuggling and the kidnapping right from the beginning, but, for whatever reason, she was targeted by her own group or by somebody close to her. When she managed to get loose, they decided it was better to take her out, but then it turns out the Uber driver most likely witnessed them killing Anna."

"Yeah, I got that far," the detective muttered, with a sigh. "I was just hoping that maybe this Madeline would know something, so we can get the ring leaders of this."

"And you think following me will get you that?"

"No, I don't," he said, glaring at him. "*You*, I still don't trust. Something is off about you."

"Sure there is something. I'm good at what I do, and you aren't sure what that means."

"No, I'm not," he muttered. "All kinds of shit is going

on around here, and I was really hoping that maybe I could get to the bottom of it."

"Maybe." Nate studied him. "Or maybe you're just trying to earn extra bonus points with somebody."

"No, but I have a cousin who got caught up in the drug trade here. He's in jail right now, but I blame the people involved. So honestly, I was just trying to get more information and to get deeper into the case, so I could find the assholes who did this to him."

"What exactly did they do to him?" Nate asked.

Manshue shrugged. "According to him, they got him hooked on drugs. Then, once he was hooked, he had to do whatever they wanted in order to keep the drugs flowing."

"Which is fairly common for any pimp," Nate noted.

"He didn't have to do anything sex related, but he was working as a mule, particularly from England and the US."

"Of course," Nate muttered. "What about Russia?"

"Russia's wild, so you can pretty well travel with whatever you want, as long as you do a half-decent job of hiding it. Then, if you do get caught, you need to pay them to get clear. Most of the officials over there are corrupt, so you can just bribe them to keep their mouths shut. It's not the same once you hit the borders here."

"Is it just drugs? Because Madeline only had one backpack."

"I wondered about that because it's not just about drugs. It involves all kinds of contraband."

"Such as?"

Manshue hesitated and then added reluctantly, "One of the big ticket items, and one that we're dealing with right now, are counterfeit diamonds."

Nate froze, then turned and stared at him. "They would

be very small to carry, something easily slipped into a backpack, and out again."

"Exactly."

Nate pondered that as they made it to the hotel. "We can certainly talk to her. But be warned, she's having a shower, and then we're heading to the morgue."

"I'll take you there," the detective offered. "Then I can bring you back here again."

And, with that, they headed upstairs to the hotel room.

CHAPTER 7

MADELINE WAS LESS than impressed to see the French detective return with Nate, but she understood his reasoning. She grabbed the clothing that he'd brought and headed to the shower. Just standing under the clean water and feeling all that nastiness drain away did an awful lot for her. Then getting dressed in clean clothes made all the difference. By the time she stepped out, she had a smile on her face. "I almost feel human again."

Nate looked up at her, smiled, then walked over to her. "Good. Now we need to head to the morgue. Are you okay with that?"

"I just want it over with," she stated fervently. "I really don't want to see a dead body, and I just know it'll be Anna. It's all too hard to understand."

"One of the things that Manshue and I discussed earlier," he began, taking a deep breath, "is that drugs and other items are quite often smuggled into the country. One of them is diamonds."

She repeated, "Diamonds?"

He nodded. "Any idea how somebody could have potentially put diamonds into your bag, so that you would have carried them through customs without knowing?"

She shook her head. "No, I have no idea. But, then again, I didn't know how easy it was for that to even happen.

Honestly, I'm floored at the idea."

"It's too easy," the detective confirmed, his accent thick and guttural, but still quite easily understandable. "And it happens way too often."

"And yet you treated me as if I were some criminal." She glared at him, finding it hard to even relax in his presence.

"I'm still not sure you're *not*," he responded in a clipped tone, "but we have three dead bodies already, and I don't want to see you end up in the morgue too."

"Thanks for that," she quipped sarcastically. "I really don't want to end up in the morgue either." She rolled her neck slowly, wishing that she could just sit down and play some mindless games to relax. She turned to Nate. "Let's go. I want this over with."

"Yep, I hear you." He turned to Brody. "Are you coming?"

"Yeah, but I'll take a different route. I'll keep in touch."

At that, the two men nodded at each other, in obvious understanding.

Madeline wondered what it meant, but then thought about her shared energy with Nate and also Brody's discussion regarding telepathy. This energy work was still a big mystery to her, so she shook off her questions.

They moved outside and into a police car, waiting for them. She stared at it, then looked back at Nate.

He smiled. "Hey, we have to get there somehow."

They got into the back seat, and the detective got into the front. The officer drove them straight to the morgue. As they got out, she looked around, wrapped her arms around herself, and muttered, "Nothing is nice about morgues, is there?"

"No, there sure isn't, but it's where we all end up."

She stared at him and winced. "That is not helpful."

"I'm a realist," Nate replied smoothly. "So it's just a fact of life."

"*Great*," she muttered. "Still doesn't make it any easier."

He laughed. "Maybe not, but it is what it is."

He was right about that, and she couldn't argue with anything at this point. They got into the main part of the building, and the detective led them downstairs, spoke to somebody on an intercom, and was led into a room with a big window. As she waited, a table or gurney of some kind on an automated system rose up, so they could see a sheet-covered body, with mirrors on the back and around the sides.

She stared at it all. "I hadn't realized it was so high-tech now."

"It has to be," the officer stated. "In this case, this is simply for identification purposes."

Meanwhile, the cover was pulled back from the dead woman's face, and Madeline stared. The grief hit her surprisingly hard merely seconds later. She gasped, then nodded. "That's Anna." Her hand covered her mouth. "It's Anna for sure." Then she noted the marks around her mouth. "I don't understand what happened to her though. She didn't have those marks on her face in the hotel room."

"It's makeup," Nate shared. "Whatever she was involved in with these men, it involved disguises. We think she was working on her next disguise, probably in the back of the Uber, but they were stopped and probably killed right then and there."

She swallowed, then stared at him. "So, the Uber driver died for absolutely no reason, outside of the fact that she escaped and got in with him?"

"That would be a good-enough reason for the kidnappers," Nate pointed out. "Plus, *escaped* means that the smugglers were in danger of being found out, and, depending on the size of this operation, that would never be acceptable to the other members of the ring."

"Right, so now we have three dead bodies, two of whom I have seen when they were alive. Do you think I'm in danger?" she asked, turning to look from Nate to the detective.

Manshue shrugged. "Everybody you have seen up until now has already been taken out," he replied. "So I'm not sure that anybody cares about you at this point, but they might try just to confirm that things are tidied up."

She shook her head. "But that's an unnecessary risk."

"Maybe, it also depends on whether they have the goods. If they think that you have their stuff still, or if they thought that Anna had stolen it and might have told you something about it," he suggested, slowly as if trying to make sense of all of it, more for him than her, "I could see them coming back after you."

She shuddered. Nate stepped closer, wrapped an arm around her shoulders, and pulled her up close. He turned to the detective. "I guess that's the trick, isn't it?"

Manshue asked, "Did Anna have contraband on her at the hotel? Maybe that's why she was so terrified."

"I think she was terrified because she thought her life was in danger," Madeline chipped in, then turned to him.

Nate nodded. "True, but, if she had tried to turn them in or to double-cross them, that makes sense as well. But that would be foolish of her, unless by getting into that Uber she was heading to somebody who would get her out of town in exchange for whatever contraband she had."

"That's possible too," Manshue admitted.

"But wouldn't they have searched her? The kidnappers are the smugglers, right? They had Anna tied up in that hotel room. Wouldn't they have searched her already?" Madeline asked, looking from one to the other. "Surely they would have, right?"

"Maybe, depending on what they thought her role in all of this was. But if they had just searched her pockets, I don't know if it would have been enough. Was there any clothing she was partial to?"

Madeline shook her head. "Not that I know of. She was in pretty rough shape. They had drugged her, at least I presume they drugged her. She seemed to have been in a drugged state."

"According to the autopsy, yes, she'd been drugged."

She nodded slowly. "So, then that part of what she told me wasn't a lie."

Nate nodded and added, "If she had the contraband with her, she would have been looking to get out. If she couldn't get out, then she would use that contraband as a way to get out. The fact that you and Anna escaped when you did meant she didn't have to pull that card."

"Did she seem as if she was waiting for something?" the detective asked.

Madeline thought about it slowly and then nodded. "Yes, but I was too, really. I was waiting for the kidnappers to come back, to find out what they wanted. I was waiting for anything to happen to explain what was going on."

"So, quite possibly, maybe she was waiting as well, but for a very different thing," Manshue offered. "Maybe she was waiting for whoever she was dealing with on the contraband, and maybe she'd been forced into it. It's all just conjecture at this point," the detective stated. "But I do know a massive smuggling ring is here that we've been trying to crack for a long time, and they don't leave behind any witnesses."

Madeline swallowed hard at that. "*Great.* I was imprisoned with her. So, if she is dead, then …"

ONCE OUTSIDE, NATE quickly ushered Madeline into the back of the same cop car, then looked over at the detective and asked, "You'll give us a lift back to the hotel, right?"

The detective nodded. "Yes, and I have a few more questions."

"Good enough," Nate agreed, "I need to get her up there and to make a plan on how to keep her safe."

"As long as nobody knows where she is, she'll be relatively safe."

"But we came out today, which means that it's possible somebody has seen us. Someone could be on the lookout for her even now." He heard her gasp beside him, as she grabbed his hand. He squeezed her hand back, then looked over at her and smiled. "It's just a chance, not a big chance though."

"But you're right, if I had just stayed inside, nobody would even know where I was." She turned and glared at the detective. "If I die because of this, that's on you."

He glared at her. "No, it's not. It's on the people who would kill you." Then he muttered something that eluded them both. "I take on way too much in my world as it is. We're just trying to solve cases."

"You need to solve this criminal activity a whole lot faster," she declared. "It's putting the tourists who come to your city in danger."

"It's not a danger that most people are exposed to, but, when it does happen, it can get pretty ugly."

"It's already happened," she muttered. "We're sitting here as proof of that."

Back up in the hotel room, she sat down on the couch and looked over at Brody, who came back just behind them. "It seems as if the coffee and the food were a long time ago."

He glanced at the trolley still in the room, with the empty dishes on it, but he nodded. "I can get some more."

Then she reconsidered that. "Actually, can we make that a pot of tea?"

He nodded, "I'll get both." He looked over at the detective. "Are you joining us?"

The detective rubbed his forehead. "Thank you. I would appreciate that." Soon they were all seated, almost as if friends, instead of the guarded relationship they had before. The detective turned to her. "Can you think of anything that Anna might have had on her, with her, that would have been out of the ordinary or that could have held diamonds?"

She blinked at that. "It never occurred to me to think of diamonds," she muttered. "You always think of drugs, not diamonds."

"Drugs are what everybody hears about, but a lot of smuggling of illegal diamonds definitely occurs all around the world. ... We're trying to stop it obviously."

"Sure," she muttered, sitting back. "Let me just think about it for a moment." Mentally she went back over the little bit that she'd seen of Anna, but it was pretty hard to see her behavior as anything other than absolute panic. "When she woke up, she was in a panic, and that was the most prevalent thing I remember. But did she have anything on her that somebody would have taken or that stood out somehow? I don't know."

"That's understandable. Anything else?"

"One thing was strange though because she was dressed in jeans and a T-shirt, and I don't think she had anything in her pockets any more than I did, yet she had her hair bundled up, like originally in a fancy updo. Now of course, after her kidnapping and sleeping, it was messy. Her hair was brown, shoulder length—at least I assumed so because of the wispy ends that I could see falling out of her bun. Everything else was normal. She had on shoes, runners, so there could have been something in the soles of her shoes, I suppose. If she wore a bra, that's probably the best way to smuggle diamonds."

The detective looked at her sharply. "Pardon?"

"They could have easily been sewn into a bra. Did they take a look at that?"

"I don't know, but I'll get them to do that." With that, the detective stood and walked a few feet away to make a quick phone call, then sat back down. "It would be nice if that was going on, but, if she still had the diamonds on her body, that meant her killer didn't get the diamonds. So these people could still be looking at Madeline here as holding their diamonds."

"If Anna's killer didn't get them from her or from my backpack—where I supposedly smuggled them through customs for the criminal ring—the kidnappers would already have the diamonds. Plus, the hotel security footage showed Anna in disguise and in a different outfit with a bag the previous night, so the kidnappers should have checked her bag too."

"Right, and, after checking all those places, the kidnappers may still be after you because they didn't get their diamonds back."

"But we don't know for sure that they're still after me or that they are still looking for their diamonds," she pointed out. "Granted, Brody and Nate are keeping me safe out of an abundance of caution. Yet there hasn't been any problems for me since I escaped. Maybe the kidnappers sent the housekeeper to let me loose on purpose because maybe the kidnappers are also working with the housecleaning woman on staff at that hotel."

"It's possible, yes." The detective nodded thoughtfully. "It's an interesting theory anyway. And then, when Anna ran, she was probably hoping to get away free and clear, whether alone or with one of the two guys who showed up at your hotel or even with the hotel housekeeper or somebody else we don't know about. So, … when you came out of the bathroom, did you sense anything between Anna and that guy?"

She frowned at him. "Now you're asking me to remember something that happened when I was still completely panicked," she murmured.

"Think about it now. You mentioned that she was in line and ready to go next."

She nodded. "Yes, she was, and they didn't seem to be talking. I didn't … There may have been some murmurings before I exited the bathroom, but I would have assumed that Anna was just asking to go to the bathroom too."

"And that is quite possibly all it was," the detective muttered. "We need to look for a connection between the two of them."

She agreed, staring at him. "That would make sense."

The detective was on it and already had his phone out, making phone calls.

Not wanting to have all the information flow in only one direction, Nate sent Terkel the same information. When Nate looked up from his phone, the detective studied him.

"Do you really expect your team to help you out in this?" he asked.

"Absolutely," Nate stated in a determined tone. "The job was to come find Madeline, and the fact that she's still not free and still not out of danger means we're staying on the job until we confirm that she is safe. Then, after this is sorted, we're taking her home to England. And, if need be, I can always bring in MI6 to help us."

The detective snorted at that. "This is hardly an MI6 issue."

"If we've got illegal diamonds being smuggled into France from England, it certainly *is* part of their jurisdiction."

At that, the detective frowned and shrugged. "We should probably alert Interpol as well."

"What will you alert them to? We don't have a face for the one remaining kidnapper we know of, and we don't have anybody else involved in this that you know of."

"That's how the smuggling rings want it, as anonymity keeps everybody safe. And the unmasked guy obviously didn't follow the rules and is now dead because of it."

"Right. And Anna is dead too. Whether or not she had anything to do with the actual smuggling and kidnapping, they both paid the price."

"Or maybe she was even doing this willingly," Madeline jumped in. "I just want to confirm that I don't end up dead as well."

"That won't happen," Nate declared. "We'll make sure of that."

"That's what you say," Madeline argued, "but you and I both know that things can go to shit sometimes, and we have absolutely no way to stop it from happening."

"Let me put it this way," Nate began, as he grabbed her hand, lacing her fingers with his. "I would do an awful lot to make sure you don't end up in the morgue with Anna. We need to find out if the diamonds were anywhere on her body or in her body," he added, with a headshake.

"The autopsy would have checked that," the detective noted.

"Our team will also check the hotel's video feed again to see if either of the two men caught on camera may have been talking to anybody else, even if out of the reach of the cameras. That could confirm another connection to even the hotel staff."

"I went through the hotel cameras," the detective shared, "and I didn't see anything. But you're right, that would be something to go back over again."

"It wouldn't even have to be a verbal contact. It could have been something smooth and simple, just a handoff or any physical acknowledgment. I have the security footage here too." At that, Nate got up, walked over to his laptop, and scrolled through the feed. He found the unmasked guard who had visited both women in the hotel room. As Nate backtracked on the video feed, he saw the man coming in through a side door, and the unmasked man had nodded up to the cameras and kept on going.

"There," Nate stated, bringing the detective to look over his shoulder. "Take a look at this." As Nate rewound the feed, with everybody standing behind him and watching, they all saw the unmasked man that Madeline saw had stopped at the outside door, the door unlocking for him, and then his stepping inside, looking up at the camera with a slight nod, almost as if to say *hello* or to send a *thank you*, then carrying on.

"So, somebody in hotel security staff is in on this," the detective declared, with quiet satisfaction on his face. "That is a link that I can chase down." He got up, put down his coffee cup, and headed out.

CHAPTER 8

"WHAT DOES THAT mean?" Madeline asked Nate, her arms wrapped around her chest.

"A reminder that we should probably change our rooms," he replied.

She stared at him. "Why? We're not at the same hotel."

He turned to face her. "We just watched a video that showed us a security guard or somebody in the security department at that hotel let in that kidnapping guy. If they've got such a contact at that hotel, chances are good that they could have a relationship of that sort with this hotel as well."

The color drained from her face, and she let out a slow breath. "So, we need a new hidey-hole then."

"Exactly." He pulled out his phone and more or less had the same conversation with Terkel.

She packed up the few possessions she had, which wasn't much. The panic crept up on her again. She wanted to toss her old clothes because who wanted the clothing that she'd survived a kidnapping in? Yet it was the only outfit she had besides what she was wearing. If she got to another hotel, she could easily wash her old clothes, and, given her current circumstances, she wouldn't look a gift horse in the mouth, since having another set of clothing to put on was a luxury at this moment.

By the time Nate got off the phone, she was ready and standing at the door.

He quickly packed up his gear too. "Terk's sending me another address in a few minutes. Good that you are all packed up. Let's go. I'll send Brody a message."

"Right," she muttered, looking around. "I didn't even realize he'd left."

"He left with the detective, mostly because he wants to be kept in the loop. Don't worry. We know what we're doing."

She raised her hands. "Maybe you do, but I don't, so pardon me if I question everything."

He laughed. "Let's go." He reached for the doorknob, then stopped and swore.

"What's the matter?"

"We're too late. They will be here soon." He spoke to her in a clipped tone. "There'll be a hell of a lot of gunfire in a few minutes, so I need you to go into the bathroom and get in the tub and stay down low. I'll see if I can hold them off."

She shook her head. "Hell no," she snapped, "that gunfire will take us all out. Much better we just run."

He opened the door and looked down the hallway. "If we get caught, … but that is a discussion for another time." He quickly stepped across the hallway, checked the nearest door, and, finding it locked, he pulled her into the stairway. "Move. We need to stay as public as possible."

With that, they kept going and finally stepped into the front lobby of the hotel and out the main door. Once outside, she took a deep breath and let her face soak in the fresh air.

"Run!"

Startled, she gasped and stood there, frozen.

Nate grabbed her hand and pulled her down the street, as if they were being chased. When he finally got her around a corner, and they could take a breath, he slowed his pace. "Okay, we have a few more blocks to go, and then we'll be at our new destination." Following the GPS on his phone, they quickly ended up at the entrance to a back alley. He stopped, checked it out quickly, and then turned into it.

"This is not at all comforting," she whispered, staring up at the back wall facing them.

He laughed. "No, it may not be, but you'll feel better once we get there." He took the nearest steps to the basement and punched in a code, then led her inside the building and kept checking something on his phone.

Opening another door, they scooted in and headed down a long, dark hallway to another door and then another. Next was a simple set of stairs, and, by the time they made their way up, she could see daylight out the landing window. The whole thing seemed bizarre to her, but they continued to follow whatever secret path he had directions for. When he came to yet another door, he looked at her and smiled. "This is it." He used another code to open the door and found themselves inside a small apartment.

She walked in and looked around. "So, does this belong to you guys or what?"

"No clue. I asked for a safe place for us, and this is what I got.'

She turned, looked at him, and smiled. "You're a handy man to have around."

He shrugged and, with a smile, clarified, "Terkel's team is handy to have around. Don't kid yourself because there is far more to this than you realize. Terk's whole team is behind us right now."

She nodded soberly. "I guess most people in trouble don't have access to the help and the security support that you guys have given me. I'm not sure how I got so lucky, but I really appreciate it."

"You got lucky because you were heading to Bullard's compound, and he feels responsible," Nate explained. "So he's doing everything he can to get you wherever you want to go safely."

She winced. "I almost feel bad about the fact that I don't want to go work for him now."

Nate laughed. "He half expected it, once he realized you work with energy."

She frowned at him. "He knows?"

"He knows, and it was one of the reasons he wanted you to come work for him. Since he's very close to Terk and the rest of us, Bullard understood you better than you think. But, once energy-working people find out that a whole team does energy work at Terkel's place, they generally want to go work with Terk's team."

She nodded. "Who wouldn't," she noted in amazement. "It would completely enhance the development of our abilities in ways that we can't even comprehend. I could choose to develop my gifts slowly or to work with others of the same mind-set and abilities to develop at a much faster rate and in so many other ways. Yeah, one choice is much better for us."

"Exactly." He smiled. "Every time Bullard comes up with anybody who has energy work available in their skill set, they all choose to go to Terkel because he's got his own hidden power source, and it comes in very handy at times."

"*All* the time," she guessed, "not just sometimes, I'll bet."

"True, but I don't know how many people you've come up against where your energy didn't work on them—or didn't work through certain circumstances, such as where you were drugged or injured or your senses were otherwise dulled. However, it happens enough times that we can't always depend on the energy alone. Otherwise, when restricted to just our normal senses, how everybody else is functioning, we feel blind."

"It is like being blind," she admitted. "I was a surgical nurse for a long time and didn't even realize that I was doing the energy work for the patients on the table, until one day I realized that I wasn't feeling very well, and something was off. I was at the OR table, but I couldn't do anything to help energywise. It was just a simple case of the surgery and the surgeons working. The patient didn't die or anything, but he certainly didn't do very well, and it took him forever to heal," she whispered, as waves of sorrow flew through her.

"Then I realized how much I was influencing the outcome and how much more I could do if I wanted to leave the standard hospital system. However, it was hard leaving the established system because I didn't know any energy workers. As a surgical nurse, I could just keep doing what I was doing, but then I heard about this job with Bullard." She shrugged. "Since he runs his own private clinic, I thought I would help more people."

"And that's quite possible. Terkel has some major energy healers on his team. The kind who can heal people no matter where they are, so they're not in danger and can work with people all over the world."

Madeline stopped and stared. "Is that even possible? Wow, I would absolutely love that," she exclaimed, "particularly if it isn't done for money. I don't think healing should just be for the rich."

"I agree. Healing should be for everybody," Nate stated, with a gentle smile. "You still need a system in place, and you have to find people who need your gift."

"People all over the world need healing," she stated, "but getting it to them? That's always been the challenge."

"I think Terk and his two healers got that part pretty-well locked down." Nate laughed. "I know they were responsible for healing a lot of their own team, who got seriously wiped out, and kept them alive while they recovered. So, if you're interested in working with Terkel, he's an option."

"Absolutely. I would love to work with Terkel," she exclaimed, then stopped. "But where is he located? I'm not sure I can even travel anymore."

"He's in England." He shot her a laughing smile. "Manchester."

"Manchester? Good God, why there?"

"My understanding is because that's where the castle is."

Her eyes lit up. "He has a castle? As in a small one or a really big one?"

"A massive castle, of a size that they'll never fill, and it's all pretty-well staffed right now. A lot of pregnant women are there too. Or maybe have already had their babies."

Madeline's eyes widened. Then she shook her head at that. "I can't imagine having babies when doing this work."

"For Terk's team, it's their life, and they want as much of a normal life as they can get, considering the skills they have," he shared. "As you already know, having these skills makes us different, and other people don't accept us. We find acceptance a hard thing to find. Yet we're all entitled to the life we want, and often energy workers meeting other energy workers makes that life possible because nobody else would love us."

"I agree with you there." Madeline went silent for a long moment, then admitted, "Having a family is not something I thought I could have, so I just put it out of my mind."

He turned to face her. "Why not? Can't you have children?"

"No idea." She shrugged. "Can't say that I've had a relationship that's lasted long enough to try. Most men think I get weird in the nighttime. Apparently I release energy while I'm sleeping. It freaks out my dates. Not that they understood, just that I don't *feel* normal to them."

He chuckled. "Pretty shallow of them."

She frowned at him. "You sat beside me while I slept, didn't you?"

"Sure. When I saw your energy slipping around, I just sent it back to your system to heal yourself." He chuckled. "Why waste it? You were struggling with nightmares. You needed some peace and calming energy in your life to help you deal with everything that was going on. It just made sense to send that energy back to you."

She blinked at him. "You told my energy to look after me?"

"Sure. Why not?" he asked, frowning. "You're looking at me as if I did something very strange."

"You did do something very strange—in a good way, but still strange. Everyone made it sound as if I were the problem."

"It is you, but it's your energy, and it's very active at nighttime or whenever you are sleeping, it seems. You just need to give it orders while you're asleep. So, you can capture it and rein it in, you know?"

She snorted. "You act as if that's absolutely normal."

"For me and a lot of people, it is, and I don't even have near the same skill level that some of Terkel's team has. It's one of the reasons why I was contemplating working for him on a more full-time basis. This is a trial run for me, to see how I like working with them."

"What do you mean?"

"I have some skills that I've rarely used, and maybe it's time I think about that." He laughed. "Terkel and his team are probably just more or less waiting for me to determine how much of this I can work with. And how willing I am to use my skills to get us out of here."

"Sounds good to me," she muttered, yawning.

"And that yawn is the first sign that you need another nap." She glared at him. "Nope, no arguments. Time to go crash and burn again. When you wake up, things will look a whole lot better."

NATE WATCHED MADELINE as she slept deeply yet again. Nate worried about the level of drugs that could still be lingering in her system and also about how she was always very tired and seemed to be constantly hungry. It could be just shock still or the stress of it all, and it could be absolutely nothing to worry about. Regardless, it made him feel even more protective. With her sound asleep, he sat down to work on some of the questions they had brought up. About ten minutes later he got a call from Brody, saying he was coming in with supplies.

Nate kept an eye on her to confirm she didn't wake up, while Brody made his entrance, and whispered to him,

"She's sound asleep."

Brody nodded. "Probably the best thing for her." He unloaded an armful of supplies. "She eats like my wife, as if she's pregnant."

"I noticed that. Maybe it's her blood sugar issues or something. Plus, she's exhausted."

"Could be due to the sheer stress of going through all this."

Nate nodded but didn't seem satisfied with that explanation.

Brody looked around. "We don't want to get too comfortable here."

"Are we moving again?" Nate asked.

"Always a chance that we were seen and followed," he murmured, "so the answer will be yes. At least for now."

"Good enough. When she wakes up, we'll eat, shower, change clothes, and move again, assuming we have a place to go to by then."

"Terkel's arranging that right now," Brody shared. "He's trying not to involve any of the governments, if we don't have to, but it'll depend on the extent of his resources at the moment." He asked Nate, "Did you find out anything?"

He pointed to his laptop. "I've been researching connections between the dead man and Anna. ... Madeline's still pretty upset about Anna's death. I think in her heart of hearts that Madeline was desperately hoping that Anna was as much a victim as Madeline had been. In the end Anna probably was, but that doesn't mean she was a victim the whole time."

"Nope," Brody replied in agreement. "I'll put up our supplies and put on some coffee, while you keep talking." He walked over to the small kitchen with his bags.

Nate explained what he'd found in his research. "We've checked the security footage available for the days before the kidnapping, and there doesn't appear to be any sign of any of the trio we have pinpointed so far. As much as I could tell, the Uber driver was not connected at all. He doesn't pop up in any way, and he doesn't seem to have any prior history with Anna that we could find with a quick initial search. I do have Terk's team doing a deep dive on those three, and we'll touch base after that."

Nate walked over to the sink to pour a glass of water. "Now, it's always possible that the driver was there waiting for Anna because he knew where she was and what she was up to, but it doesn't feel right, not with the facts as we know them right now."

"No, it doesn't, and I agree. I don't think the driver's got anything to do with the smuggling ring. Of course we'll keep him on our radar to confirm that we don't overlook anything."

"Other than that, we're checking a few other events, but I'm trying to dig into Anna's history. I found a couple people in her past that she'd shown up with on street cams and social media and the like, although there isn't a whole lot of that in the last six months."

"We may have to expand our search to other countries," Brody suggested.

"I was just talking to Terkel about that," Nate added, with a nod. "And the question I'm really waiting on is from the morgue."

"Right, and that is a very different story."

When Nate's phone rang a few minutes later, he put down his coffee and answered it, facing Brody as he did. "Detective, what can I do for you?"

"You were right about one thing," Manshue replied, his voice tired. "I've just come back from the morgue. Anna had on a hairpiece, so her brown hair was a fake. Seems her long dark hair from the previous night was her real hair. Anyway her black hair was covered with glitter or black glass or something. Turns out, when they ran them through the proper checks, they were diamonds."

"So, she had diamonds in her hair? How did that work?"

The detective groaned. "Something about the diamonds were secured in some hairnet decorative thing and looked just like cut glass. I didn't see it so can't fully describe it."

"All right," Nate replied, "which means that whoever's involved in the smuggling ring didn't get their goods."

"Exactly," the detective agreed, "and now they're surely pissed and probably looking at Madeline, thinking she has their diamonds."

"Unless you get it out into the media that Anna had the diamonds on her," Nate snapped. "That might help keep Madeline safe."

"I'll approach my captain about that," the detective replied. "In the meantime, we have to rethink this case."

"Right, not smuggling drugs after all."

"No, it appears to be diamonds. Now the question really is, are you sure Madeline doesn't have any too?"

"No, I'm not, but we'll talk about it and check with her. She's sound asleep at the moment. The visit to the morgue today was pretty hard on her. The thought that Anna, who seemed to be kidnapped along with Madeline, might have been involved in the whole matter has been a shock that Madeline's not taking very well."

"Of course not. Nobody wants to think of themselves as being duped," he murmured. "Anyway, that's all I have for the moment. So get some sleep, and I'll talk to you in the morning." And, with that, the detective rang off.

Nate filled in Brody on the details and pondered the situation. "What are the chances that Anna was thinking she could double-cross a smuggling ring and run away with the diamonds and get a fresh start somewhere?"

"That would be my thought as well." Brody sat down on the chair beside Nate. "She may have been forced into this, and maybe it wasn't something she wanted to do, or she picked up a role in it somewhere along the line and got greedy. I could see that maybe she and the unmasked guy thought this was a fast and easy run, and they could get in and out with the diamonds and start fresh somewhere else, where they wouldn't ever be found."

"It's that *wouldn't ever be found* part that always gets me," he muttered. "They always seem to think that, even in today's hi-tech world, they'll somehow get away with it."

"Then it just gets worse and worse because, once they're found, they're immediately considered guilty by their fellow partners in crime. Anna obviously didn't make it very far. Whether that was because of the Uber driver or someone else, I don't know."

"Exactly," Nate agreed, "and we don't know at this point. We need more answers. In order to do that, we must find out who was working with Anna. So I was trying to get into the airport security feed to see who else may have been at the airport and showed an interest in Madeline and her travel bag. For that matter, Anna could have been scoping out the airport too. I figure she retrieved the diamonds from Madeline's bag and hid them from the two kidnappers. Of course the diamonds were not found and that led to Anna's being kidnapped as well."

"Oh, that's a good line to tug too because somebody seemed focused on Madeline and her travel bag at the Paris airport, from what she can remember anyway." Brody sipped his coffee. "I wonder what they coated the diamonds with?"

"Something to disguise them, or something to make it hard to determine what they were," Nate added.

Brody nodded. "I'm sure it won't be hard to sort out later, but the criminals are always one step ahead of us, no matter what. That just blows me away. The minute we figure out one thing, they come up with another way to carry out their bullshit."

Nate snorted. "Isn't that the truth."

Brody looked over him. "You haven't had much sleep. I suggest you try to get at least four hours, if you can."

"Absolutely, particularly if we're moving." He stood and tossed back the rest of his coffee.

Brody pointed at the laptop, a question in his eyes.

"Have at it," Nate said. "If you come up with anything important, wake me up."

"We will probably be on the move sooner than we think, so grab the sleep now, and I'll worry about waking you up if and when we get any news."

With that Nate headed toward Madeline's bedroom, once again stopping in the doorway to confirm she was okay.

"You might as well just stay in there," Brody suggested in a smooth tone. "Then I'll know where you both are. Otherwise you'll be going back and forth, checking on her. Besides, you know that's where you want to be anyway."

Nate poked his head out with a frown.

"Hey, you can't fool me." Brody tossed him a bright grin.

Nate knew he was right.

"Besides, the energy positively crackles around the two of you, so resistance is futile."

"Yeah, I don't think she's at all interested."

At that, Brody shook his head. "You're smarter than that. You know you can read the energy just as well as I can."

Nate shrugged. "Yet I've been deliberately *not* reading her energy, due to the circumstances."

"Sure, circumstances and all that are a great way to keep things in check, but not so great when considering other things you should be worrying about. And right now keeping her close is definitely a good job for you."

"I don't want to overstep any boundaries with energy, you know?"

"Yeah, and I already know you did that once, and I agreed with the reason for it then."

"And I haven't done it since."

"And yet what happens if you lose something special just because you're not willing to take a step forward?"

Nate glared at him. "Then I lose something special, I guess. It's never happened before."

"It's happening now, so you might want to keep that in mind. Plus, she's using her magic energy on me, like some helicopter mom." When Nate frowned, Brody shrugged. "Could explain some things."

With that ending note to their conversation, and some restless thoughts, Nate headed into Madeline's bedroom, curled up beside her, and slept.

CHAPTER 9

MADELINE ROLLED OVER and came up against a large, warm body. Her eyelids flew open, and she realized that Nate was curled up beside her. She smiled at that, wrapped an arm around his waist, and snuggled in. When he whispered against her ear, she shifted ever-so-slightly, so she could hear him better. "Hey," she muttered, yawning, "you're awake."

"I am, and I've been thinking about getting up and moving for the last few minutes, but a lot can be said for being curled up like this."

"It's cozy," she murmured. "If we didn't have all this shit going on in our lives, I might even consider another activity." She felt him stiffen, and she laughed. "It's okay. I'll be gentle."

At that, he gave a loud snort, then flipped them both, and she found herself suddenly on her back, staring up at him. Nate was propped on his elbows above her. "You might be gentle," he murmured, as he nuzzled his nose against hers, "but nobody claimed I would be."

She laughed. "You might come across as a big badass in life, but I think you're just a big softie on the inside." He frowned at that, making her smile even more. "See? Even the very thought of being considered a softie damages your ego. You have a certain image to uphold, after all."

"Hey, it's not so much about image," he protested, "but lots of other things are going on right now, and I certainly wouldn't want to head in that direction under these circumstances."

"That's why I mentioned it," she clarified. "You have a tendency to keep yourself ever-so-slightly separated from everything else going on, and I wanted to add something happier to the mix." He shook his head at that, but she nodded. "You absolutely do. I'm not sure why, but I suspect that it probably has something to do with that overdeveloped bloody sense of honor of yours." The voltage of his glare deepened, making her giggle.

Immediately a smile cracked his face. "How am I supposed to glare you into submission"—he chuckled—"if you're making me laugh?" Her own giggles got louder. He shook his head and added, "On that note, as much as I very much want to stay here in this very delightful position, I'll get up and go put on some coffee."

Her eyes widened, and she sat upright in shock. "You mean we have coffee, and you didn't tell me?"

"You were too busy laughing at me," he declared, faking his wounded dignity.

She snorted. "Yeah, well, get used to it. I want a lot of laughter in my life. It seems there hasn't been a whole lot of that lately, and I want laughter back."

"That is an excellent goal to consider." Nate sat up and shifted to the side of the bed. He rolled his shoulders and murmured, "I really could use a few days of rest."

"Exactly." She shook her head. "All of this has been way too much."

"And yet," he added, smiling at her, "you're doing really well."

She shrugged. "I'm not so sure about that. I think I'm adapting, but it's a transition I'm not particularly sure I want to make."

"In what way?" he asked curiously.

"If you think about it, … it's partly being adaptable but partly just adjusting to the horrible circumstances."

"You've done remarkably well, considering how crappy the circumstances are."

She patted him gently on the cheek and nodded. "You're a nice guy." He stiffened at that and then glared at her, setting her off once again in a fit of giggles.

He shook his head. "As much as I enjoy hearing that giggle and realizing that you're doing so much better, it would be nice if you would stop insulting me," he teased in a grim tone, yet he could not stop laughing, as he hopped up and walked over to the bathroom.

She was still smiling when he came back out again. Now she was up, dressed, and ready to roll. "Will we stay here long?" she asked him.

"No, not long at all."

Immediately she stilled and studied him. "Dang, I figured that we were safe here."

"And you figured wrong," he replied. "We're not exactly sure what we're up against, but let's go get some coffee and give Brody a chance to catch some sleep if he wants."

"Right, so basically we have to stand watch even though we're in a safe house?"

"Absolutely, because one never knows when a safe house is no longer safe." He walked straight to the kitchen and put on fresh coffee, leaving her standing here, his words hitting her hard.

It was a safe house until it was no longer safe.

She had just let herself believe that they *were* safe. Taking a deep breath, she turned to face Brody, who was eyeing her with a quizzical look. She shrugged. "Nate just told me how a safe house can no longer be safe anymore. I had fooled myself into thinking that our chances were good and that we were out of danger. However, now I think maybe not so much."

"No, maybe not. We had a few developments while you were sleeping."

"Anything helpful while I was down?" Nate called out from the little kitchenette.

"No, not really," Brody answered. "I expect to hear from the detective first thing."

"It's only been a few hours."

"I know, and, given only those few hours, we probably have three more before he's up and mobile. So I'll go grab some sleep while I can." And, with that, Brody headed into the second bedroom and closed the door.

She looked over at Nate. "It's not an easy life for you guys, is it?"

"Though it's not really hard either," he noted. "After all, we get to meet all kinds of people."

She smiled at that, but it felt off, wrong somehow. It wasn't that he was being distant, but it was a reminder that maybe he had this same relationship with other people who he worked with. That was an errant thought, but it still hurt somewhat.

As if sensing her mood had shifted, he walked closer and held out a hot cup of coffee. "What's that look for?"

She winced. "Nothing, just foolishness."

But he wouldn't let it go, staring at her steadily. "Clear communication really is important right now."

"No, it's not that important," she protested, trying to back away from the topic. "It was just a foolish thought on my part."

"Meaning?" he asked, his tone insistent.

She glared at him. "You could just let it go, you know?"

"I could," he replied. "Yet an awful lot is going on between us, and I don't want a problem to come up later that I didn't know about when I should have, especially considering it could change the way I make decisions."

"In other words, it's all about work," she stated, her voice tight.

His eyebrows shot up. "I'm not saying that," he said, "but obviously something special is developing between us that I wasn't expecting."

She eyed him, feeling some of her tension ease back, and asked, "Do you mean that?"

"Sure I do. Why?" he asked.

"It just occurred to me that …" Then unsure again, she backed off. "It's just … It's foolish."

"I want to hear it, foolish or not," he told her. "In order to keep problems to a minimum, clear and concise communication is required."

"Sure, but thinking about you on other jobs, meeting other people, maybe this is how you react to all the people you work with, to all the women you rescue."

His eyebrows shot up, and, for a moment, it seemed he was trying to hold back a laugh.

She glared at him. "Don't you dare laugh at me," she snapped. "Otherwise I'll never tell you what I'm thinking."

Immediately his smile disappeared, and he nodded. "And that would be fair too," he murmured, "but let me reassure you that this thing between us is not something I've ever experienced before. It's definitely not something I expected, and I do *not* travel the world rescuing pretty women. This job is really not that way at all. More often than not, the people we work with aren't female, and, if they are, they're married and have been kidnapped because their husbands wouldn't do the awful thing the kidnappers wanted them to do or some other godforsaken thing. They're victims in trouble, and that's it."

"Oh."

"I tried to point it out earlier how obviously something special is between us. I'm not sure what it is or how to handle it, and that's why I'm trying to keep a little bit of distance between us," Nate explained, hoping that she understood him. "And frankly it's not that easy to stay away from you."

She walked closer. "I'm glad to hear that, and now I do feel foolish for even bringing it up."

"That brings us back to the *don't feel foolish* conversation because we're better off to have things out in the open."

She gave him a wicked grin. "Sure, as long as we both realize that it's unnerving and difficult to bring up this relationship stuff, especially when we don't know exactly where we stand."

"Also because of the energy that's flowing around the place amid these circumstances and that I am part of the team who helped rescue you," he added, "I'll always be a little worried and uncertain."

"What do you mean?" she asked, sitting sideways on the couch and pulling her knees up against her chest.

"Because your own feelings are likely to be completely unique and no doubt affected by the circumstances of what's going on here. Plus, I don't want you to confuse being grateful as something else. I don't want you to think that you'll be safer if you end up in a relationship with me because that's not how relationships are supposed to be built, and I would do a lot to avoid it. The same way that I wouldn't want you to choose to marry someone based on the amount of money they may have in the bank."

"Oh." She stared at him in fascination. "None of that ever occurred to me, not once."

He gave her a lopsided grin. "Now that's a good thing for me, but it would be very understandable on your part."

"Understandable," she repeated, as if rolling that concept around on her tongue. "I can see that, if you do this rescue work all the time, it could be a fairly troublesome reaction. I guess some women throw themselves at you just because, *huh?*"

"Nope, never been in that position." He flashed her a wicked grin. "Though I can't say that I would have turned it down—in the past, you know."

She gave him a big eye roll and chuckled at his exaggerated tone. "Sure, sure, now you're talking the big talk."

He burst out laughing. "It's just talk because I don't play with my heart or somebody else's. It's a completely different story if you're in a relationship intended to be temporary fun for the moment, and then we're both happy to leave it. However, all too often, they aren't like that."

"No, I would imagine they aren't," she murmured. "I have mixed feelings about those myself. Every once in a while, you end up wondering if you should have made it not quite so impermanent and left a bit of an option there for growing forward together," she shared. "That happened once, with somebody I fell further in love with than I had expected to ..." She gave a small laugh. "Let's just say it was a sobering realization to see that I might have wanted the relationship to grow into something more, but he had no wish to take things any further. I stopped doing those short-term relationships after that. Once I let a man into my bed, I have major feelings for him," she admitted. "And, when those feelings aren't returned, … it sucks."

"It can suck," he agreed. "Good for you for understanding that it wasn't something you are good with."

"Absolutely. It's a hard thing to pull back on, you know?"

He nodded. "All relationships are hard to go backward on. It's as if we have this permanently broken Reverse button."

She smiled, picked up her cup of coffee, and took a sip. "We're already doing more talking than I'm used to, which is good."

"I prefer more communication over not enough. If the relationship is crazily, wildly passionate, and the communication comes afterward, that's fine too."

Even the very thought of that made her heart race.

"Then there is the energy factor added to us. I've used my energy to help you deal with some of this, so you're connected to my energy already," he shared, his voice calm and patient.

"I guess you have used energy to keep me safe and to keep yourself safe, and that could be a potential issue." She studied him. "I've never had a relationship with anybody who could even talk energy, much less understand and work with it."

"That's another hazard of the trade, isn't it?" he asked, with a nod. "So many people don't know what they could do with these gifts. They seem to run energy and use it completely comfortably, without having a postmortem on it," he noted, "and that's always fascinating to me."

"Of course. It would be to me too," Madeline confirmed. "It's pretty amazing to think about what people can do with energy. I think the postmortem comes more into play when two parties are involved in sharing a long-term mutual relationship. Otherwise, if it's just someone learning and experiencing what their special skills can do, then engaging in the energy work can be awesome on its own."

Nate nodded. "But when they apply themselves and can really harness that energy, it is freaking unbelievable. That's one of the reasons why going to Terkel's place and working with him and his team is so important to me. I dare say, it's also why it was important for Bullard to see if you could work with his group."

She chuckled. "My energy healing is something I do automatically. Working with it all the time makes me wonder what more I can do, where I could learn more about how to utilize it. I sure don't know enough," she muttered. "I understand that Bullard knows, but I'm really not anxious to travel."

"I know he feels terrible about this happening to you while you were traveling to his clinic," he reminded her. "I hope you don't hold him responsible. He's really a great guy."

"Oh, gosh no, I absolutely don't hold him responsible at all. This was one of those U-turns in life that you take because circumstances showed you another path. I don't know quite where that U-turn will take me. I just know that Africa doesn't seem to be a good fit for me anymore."

NATE DIDN'T KNOW what to say to her at that point, but he was trying to be as honest as he could. When his phone rang, he checked his screen. "Terkel, what's up?" he asked.

"Just heard from the detective about the diamonds," he murmured. "Did you tell her?"

"I haven't yet."

"Do it now, and then we need answers to some questions. She may have to go back down to the police station."

When the conversation was over, she looked at him, her gaze wide. "What was that about diamonds?"

With a fresh cup of coffee in hand, he sat down with her and explained what the forensic people had found in Anna's hair.

The color blanched from her face as she stared at him. "Good God," she murmured. "So she took the stash from my bag and decided to steal from the smuggling ring?"

Nate grimaced. "Probably so."

"But how did she hide it from her partners in crime? Her hair was down in the earlier cam footage with that first guy. Were the diamonds already there?"

"We don't know for sure, not based on the quality of the security feed. Her hair was shiny, and the diamonds were also black. Seems she painted them."

"Can you paint diamonds?" she asked.

"Presumably Anna found some way to do it, but I don't know firsthand," he shared, with a shrug. "Where there's a will, there's a way, I guess."

"Always," she murmured. "This is not something we want to be involved in."

"That's why the cops didn't believe your story at first and why we couldn't understand why—because they didn't let us in on the smuggled diamonds element. Now the bigger problem is, if the cops are thinking that, then what are the smugglers thinking? If the smugglers didn't get their diamonds, but they have your bag, and you were kept with Anna, they could imagine how she might slip you the diamonds. Anna taking the diamonds from your bag is what we think got you into trouble in the first place and is what ended up getting Anna killed."

"Oh my God." Madeline bolted to her feet and started to pace. "That's what this is all about, isn't it? The cops *and* the smugglers think I have the diamonds." She turned to face him, stunned at this turn of events. "To even think I do or worry that I do is bad news." She stopped, picked up her coffee, and stared out the window. "I can't believe that I didn't have a clue," she muttered. "I feel so stupid."

"How would you have known?" he asked. "What would be your clue that you were in the midst of a diamond smuggling operation?"

She blinked. "Right. ... It's probably even more foolish to think I would have known rather than be oblivious, isn't it?"

"Maybe."

"God." She scrubbed her face with her free hand. "I'm a mess. I'm a freaking mess. I can't even think clearly."

"You're doing fine."

She turned and glared at him. "Would you have known they were diamonds?"

He frowned, then shook his head. "I probably wouldn't have had a clue. I don't understand or even pay any attention to most hair contraptions that women use to begin with," he admitted. "So, painting and then hiding black diamonds in her black hair as a disguise is a very smart one, in my layperson's opinion."

"It was a pretty good place for Anna to hide them, wasn't it?" She sat down, casting her mind back. "She was only alone in that hotel bathroom for a minute or so. She came out and seemed to have run her fingers through her hair—which was a wig we now know—and washed her face, and so did I, right? We were just trying to get through the kidnapping nightmare."

"So, she still had the diamonds at that point, and that was her *get out of jail free* card," he muttered, "but she was trying to do it in such a way that she didn't have to give them up. Getting out of jail free is one thing, but having enough money to go live a new life somewhere safe, and not have to be a smuggler, that was a whole different story."

"Do you think she was forced into it?" she muttered.

"I don't know. That's a part of her history that we don't have here. All I can say is, at the end of the day, she had the diamonds, and she chose not to hand them over, even after her own partners in crime had drugged her and had held her against her will. That tells us she was desperately trying to get out of her association with them."

"That explains why she was so terrified, much more than I was, and that makes more sense now too. She had the diamonds on her, so she was terrified of either being caught double-crossing them, or of losing the diamonds."

"Did she appear to be …" Nate hesitated, looking for the right word.

"What?" Madeline asked curiously. "I didn't see her awake for very long, and I didn't know her that well."

"Did she seem to be somebody who could take care of herself in the world? I mean, all alone, without anybody's help?"

Madeline pondered that. "She was so freaked out and so

panicked, the same as I was, only a bit worse, that I'm not sure I can even answer that question," she told him. "It's one thing to consider somebody in the light of waking up to find themselves a captive, but to now know that she had the diamonds and was smart enough to get away from that scenario with them? Well, … obviously she knew more than I did."

He smiled at that. "Yet you both got away, whether the housekeeper alone was an element the kidnappers didn't consider or maybe because your unmasked visitor had a soft spot for women and wasn't up for the whole kidnapping part of their smuggling ring."

"We won't know because, gee, look at that. … He's dead too," she noted sarcastically, "and that inability to kidnap women may be why. But he can't talk, and he can't explain himself. So it's up to us to fill in the pieces, as much as we can."

"I had been searching whether the dead guy, your unmasked visitor, had any prior relationship with Anna. Maybe they were in this together."

"Which would make the most logical sense for letting us go, whether he had the housekeeper do it or not. Still, if Anna had the diamonds on her, and he knew that too, it also makes sense. But why let me go then? Why not just escape with her or pretend to get knocked out or something?"

"If Anna was working for or with him, he could tell the smuggling ring that he didn't understand what had gone wrong. Meanwhile he could let her go because why wouldn't he, when she was working with them to begin with, and had the diamonds on her person? Still, it was taking a big risk when you make solo decisions that the other smugglers won't like."

Madeline grimaced. "Often when you think you know who you're working with, that risk is mitigated because you believe that you'll pull it off and that nobody will know. In this case, obviously something went wrong. And it could just as easily have been what the criminals also saw on the security cameras, since our dead guy knew that somebody in the hotel security crew was in on the kidnapping event. So do we have any idea who that was yet?"

"No, the detective is supposed to be chasing that down."

She rolled her eyes at that one. "I suppose he hasn't gotten back to you on that?"

"No, he hasn't, not on that issue, but I expect to hear from him anytime though, based on what Terk told me." Nate glanced at his phone again.

"*Great*, I was hoping we could skip that whole *meet with the cops* thing for a while."

"Potentially we can for a bit." He looked over at her. "But, at the end of the day, somebody has to have answers, and somebody'll have to confirm faces, and, in this case, that somebody is you."

She winced. "I've confirmed Anna's dead face, and that is enough," she muttered. "I would be totally okay to not go to any more morgues." He didn't say anything to that but got up and poured her a fresh cup of coffee. She sighed as she stared down at the cup. "Makes me sound so entitled, doesn't it?"

He sighed. "No, you just want this mess to go away, but it won't go away very easily, and, for now, it's just become part and parcel of us. We will do all we can, but I'm not saying there'll be any easy answers, or any answers soon enough."

"There haven't been any so far, so I guess I'm not surprised."

He smiled at her. "How about some breakfast?"

"Is there food?" She bounded up to look at the grocery bags, still sitting on the counter, but they were empty now.

"We have some. Keep in mind that we might have to move again on short notice."

"Right," she muttered. "Another thing I so don't want to hear."

He ignored her with the buzzing of text messages coming now on his phone. "So, that was the detective. He wants a follow-up meeting, but, barring that, he wants a phone conversation."

"So why is he texting you? Why not just call?"

"He was waiting to see if we were awake," he noted. "You know, he's invoking some courtesy now that they know you don't have the diamonds." She snorted, but Nate quickly called the detective. "Most of us are up. I've got you on Speakerphone, and Madeline is here with me. She says to the best of her knowledge she doesn't have any diamonds, and she didn't have anything to do with the diamonds in the first place. She also didn't know that Anna had diamonds in her hairpiece. And, yes, I do believe her."

The detective didn't say anything for a moment. "I guess that would make sense. The fewer people in the know, the better."

"I don't know what the street value is for something like that," Nate pointed out, "but I imagine it's thousands if not hundreds of thousands of dollars."

"Try millions," Detective Manshue stated, his tone harsh. "I've just come from forensics, and they're still running it down, but that's their current guess."

"*Great*, so if the smugglers think Madeline has them,

they won't give up very easily."

"No, they sure won't, so it's even more important that you keep her safe."

"I was planning on it, but, yeah, I get it," Nate replied in a sarcastic tone of voice.

Taking advantage of the awkward pause in the conversation, Madeline asked, "Detective, are you anywhere close to figuring out who did this? I really want my life back—the sooner, the better."

"I'm sure you would," he replied, "but, if you don't have any information for us, any further investigation won't be easy."

"No, of course it won't," she muttered. "But since I didn't have anything to do with it, I have no information to give you."

"Maybe not, maybe you're just the unlucky person who got picked to move their contraband."

"So did all the diamonds that Anna had in her possession come from my bag alone? How many can they move at a time?" she asked.

"These are fairly well-funded missions," he muttered. "They may have used more than one mule."

She stopped and looked back at Nate. "Do you think Anna stole my bag?" There was silence as both men contemplated that.

Nate turned to her. "Did you ever see Anna before?"

She pondered that question for a bit. "First, Anna was using disguises, as we now know. Second, I wasn't on alert to look for criminals and don't remember who I saw on the plane or on the bus or even at the airport. Third, I believed her when she told me that she had just left her boyfriend's place and had gone for coffee. ... Why wouldn't they have just grabbed my bag at the airport?" she asked. "I don't understand that."

"Did you give them a chance?"

"Or maybe that was Anna's job, and she missed her chance. Or maybe she did and then …"

"Then what?"

"She was wearing that auburn wig when she was kidnapped, *with* her stolen diamonds affixed to her real hair underneath that wig, or so I presume. From what the forensics people have told you, her real hair is long and black and shiny. Also forensics found the diamonds, painted black, on some hair extension or whatnot amid her real hair, right? The wig took some planning, and she needed the time to paint and to affix the diamonds to some hairpiece, right? So her kidnapping disguise may have been how she planned to escape from the smuggling ring. Instead she gets kidnapped."

"So, in that case," the detective began, "let's say she was probably moving those diamonds on her own, but maybe she decided she needed a second score in order to really get out of town."

"That's possible too," Nate noted slowly. "Can you check the buses leaving the airport and see if she got on one of them?"

"Yeah, right, I'll do that now. If she was the one who took Madeline's bag, that would be an interesting angle."

"I don't know about an *interesting* angle," she replied, "but it would make sense why she was grabbed and later held with me. Maybe they thought she was trying to run away, and she didn't get a chance to explain herself."

Nate looked over at her and sighed. "You're still trying to make her into a good person."

She glared at him. "I'm not sure that she's *not* a good

person," she claimed, "and I realize in these circumstances there is often more to the story. I just think we need to understand more before we automatically condemn her."

He gently held her hand. "You're right. There could be a lot more to her story, and the reality is that she may have been forced into this industry and just wanted out. You're on her side, and I get that."

"It's hard not to be. I was in that room with her, and she was tied up just like me and just as terrified, if not more so."

He nodded. "I'm not surprised that she was terrified. If you think about it, if she had blackmailed the smuggling ring or had betrayed them in some way, she had every right to be terrified."

Madeline groaned. "You're back to thinking that Anna did it on purpose, aren't you?"

"This last part of it, yes. I think she was trying to get out, and this was her way, or at least her attempt, but it failed. Something happened that she wasn't counting on. Odds are that the organization was more sophisticated than she realized and that more layers of people were watching Anna than she knew of."

"Was her boyfriend the man who died at the hotel?"

"That would also make sense, but somebody else was involved too, somebody associated with hotel security, and that's someone who we have to find."

"Right. My vote is for the security guard at the hotel at the time they brought me in, all drugged up," she stated.

"We've already got a list of names which we're tracking down," the detective shared over the phone, almost startling her that he was still in on the conversation. "We'll find him."

"What are the chances you'll find him in a dumpster though?" she muttered.

"Unfortunately it's quite possible. They seem to be cleaning up and taking out anybody involved, even witnesses, when they only had a problem with Anna. So you can bet nobody'll be given a free pass."

Nate added, "But it depends on how much value the people bring to the organization and whether they can prove that they still have that value."

"In this case," the detective replied, "the security guard's position has been compromised. Because of the head nod, the silent interchange involving the one guy who is already dead, we knew somebody was involved in hotel security, so that puts him in jeopardy already. By the time we find him, he may already be dead."

"Yeah, so do you have anybody who didn't show up for work lately?" Nate asked. "With their recent actions, he probably is dead already."

"I agree. So far, we don't have a body, but we do have two people we're still trying to locate. I'm waiting to hear back from the team on them."

"Keep us posted," Nate replied and disconnected. As soon as the phone conversation was over, Nate looked over at Madeline, but his phone rang again.

She groaned. "Jesus, even here we can't get any peace and quiet, can we?"

He chuckled. "Terkel, what's up?"

"Get a move on."

"Ah, shit," he muttered, bolting to his feet, even as he saw Brody racing out of the bedroom. Nate turned to her, and she was already taking the coffee cups to the counter and putting on her shoes.

"Grab any of your personal stuff from the bathroom and the bedroom," he reminded her. "We have less than two minutes to get out."

"Okay, where are we going?"

"We'll talk once we're out of the building. In the meantime, open up all your senses so we can keep this moving smoothly." With that, he quickly raced to the door, where Brody stood, ready and waiting. Nate nodded as Madeline approached. He looked over at Brody. "We ready?"

"Yep." Brody stepped out first, with the two of them following closely behind. They raced down to the ground floor in the same convoluted manner she remembered from their arrival.

"Why is this building so complex?" she muttered.

"For exactly the same reason we're using it, to keep people away."

"How funny that it didn't work today."

"Actually it did. What we don't want is to have them come in, with guns blazing."

"The thing that's bothering me is, how are they tracking us?" she asked in awe.

"I don't know, and that's one of the things we must figure out, but right now is not the time." And, with Brody and Nate pushing her forward faster and faster, they ended up hitting the street level and were outside, where they suddenly slowed to a fast walk.

"How is it we don't look as if we're absolutely running for our lives," she muttered.

He laughed. "To some people it probably does look like that, and, to others, it seems as if we're just out having a fun day in the sun," he muttered. "People see what they want to see."

"You know what I want to see? I want to see an airplane that's ready to take me back to England," she muttered.

"Preferably now."

"If it weren't for the cops, believe me that I would have you there already."

"What difference does it make with the cops?" she asked, turning to face him. "Why don't we just go? It's not as if the detective has anything on me. I haven't done anything. I should be cleared to just pack up and go. Of course I don't have my passport yet, … so that is a problem."

Nate's phone rang while they were walking quickly toward God-only-knows what end. "Look, Detective. We have our own problems here right now. Our position has been compromised, so we're on the move. You need to stop thinking of her as being a part of this. I need to get her out of here and somewhere safe."

"Do not leave the country," the detective warned.

She snatched the phone from Nate's hands, clearly hearing Detective Manshue's words. "Why not?" she asked in a harsh tone. "Do you want to see me end up like Anna, her partner, and that Uber driver?" she asked bitterly. "It's not as if you're offering me any protection. I wanted to be a guest in your city, not in the city morgue."

"Give the phone back to the man," Manshue ordered.

She glared at it but handed the cell back over to Nate. "Gee, what a surprise. He wants to talk to the men," she muttered.

Nate just gave her a look. "What's up, Detective?"

"I understand that you're trying to get her back home again, but we can't have her leaving just yet. We'll need her as part of this case, and we need her as a witness."

"And that's just fine," he agreed. "You can have her as part of the case, and we can always fly her back again for any court testimony, if that's required. But, right now, we need to keep her safe, so she'll actually be alive for that."

"The problem is, they've got to think she still has the diamonds, and that's a whole different problem."

"She doesn't have the diamonds. Forensics does."

"Unless Madeline was just one part of the smuggling operation this time. What if Anna had somebody else's diamonds? The smugglers may well be looking for a second mule's stash of diamonds. Word on the street is that the smugglers are offering a reward for those."

"So tell them you've got them."

"The problem is, the smugglers are missing more diamonds than forensics recovered. So we're checking Anna's movements on the city buses and her last known locations. We've checked everything."

"Then the second stash was dumped, or the bus driver found it and never turned it in, or Anna snagged it too and hid one set while she worked on disguising the second set."

"We couldn't find anything," the detective muttered in frustration.

"So maybe Anna had another partner, not dead, that she probably handed off the second stash of diamonds, and Madeline's backpack, with the first stash removed from it, has now been deep-sixed in some dumpster bin somewhere along the line."

"Maybe," he muttered.

"Look, when we get to another location, I'll contact you. I can't talk now." And, with that, Nate disconnected, then looked over at Brody. "Do you have anybody on Terk's team who can find lost items?"

Brody chuckled. "We do have somebody who can tell us simple directions—go left, turn right. And we do have people who can camouflage us. All of those are options that we may have to call on, and we can get them to help us with that. But, as you know, the more we use our gifts, if anybody else out there is using energy, we attract their attention too. And we don't want to do that too often because the bad guys can be energy workers too. Plus, it drains our own people if they're on other cases. But I've already contacted our finder, Langdon. He'll get back to us pronto."

"Got it, but we're fast becoming a problem."

"We absolutely are," Brody agreed. "We have a smuggling ring putting a target on Madeline's back. I can ask if anybody can find lost items specifically because that would be a hell of a good ability to have."

"Wouldn't it though," Nate muttered, looking back at Madeline, who was struggling. "We need to grab a vehicle."

"Yeah, I was thinking that too. A mall is up ahead. I'll meet you there in five." And, with that, Brody took off at a run, catching a streetlight and crossing so it seemed to be a completely natural move on his part.

"Now where is he going?" she asked warily, as she slowed at the stop sign.

"To get us some wheels." Nate looked at her in concern.

"I'm fine," she muttered. "Totally fine."

"Are you though?"

"Sure, why not?"

"So, tell me something, and be honest. Are you always this out of breath?"

She glared at him. "Meaning, am I this out of shape? Is what you are asking?"

"No, that's not what I asked," he clarified. "*Out of breath*. Are you this out of breath all the time?"

She stopped to think about it and shrugged. "I don't know that I am. Why?"

"I just wondered if something else is going on because you've been out of breath quite a bit on this op. Plus, you are still sleeping a lot. And you're not pregnant, right?" When she frowned at him, he added, "Normally I would think these are side effects to the drugs, but they should be out of your system by now," he explained. "You're the nurse. Isn't that right?"

She shrugged. "Generally, yes. If you want more detailed answers, I need the name of the drugs."

"Terk got them for me, so I can show you that text later."

She groaned. "As a nurse, I should have asked to see the test results at the hospital."

He smiled, then swung an arm around her shoulders and casually walked her across the street. "You were distressed. Plus, we couldn't very well leave a forwarding address, now could we? Regardless, we can figure that out later. Now please smile," he said. "The last thing I want is anybody to think that I'm forcing you to be with me."

"*Great*," she muttered. "That's the last thing I want at this point too."

"Now, the question is, if somebody is after us, how are they finding us?"

"I wondered that myself. But short of their being able to track us, they would have to follow us. Otherwise I don't know how and why."

"When you were in the airplane, did you have any interactions with anyone?"

She looked at him. "What do you mean? Of course I did. Flight attendants, various passengers, the lady beside me."

"The lady beside you? Who was she?"

"Just a lady beside me on the plane. We were in economy class, and she wasn't impressed. Something about her husband, complaining how he supposedly booked her a better flight and a better seat, but he didn't. It was a running joke during the whole flight because she couldn't believe she was in economy."

"Did she look like someone who would normally be in business class?" When Madeline stopped, he nudged her forward. "Keep walking," he whispered. "Let's not attract any attention."

She walked carefully forward, her thoughts obviously elsewhere. When they got to the other side of the street, she replied, "You know something, she didn't."

"Didn't what?"

"She didn't look to be somebody in business class."

"Okay. So, if she wasn't, did she show an inordinate amount of interest in you?"

Madeline shook her head. "Not really. We were just seatmates, and we were having a decent conversation, the way you do to pass the time with strangers." He nodded and didn't say anything. "Why are you asking that?"

"If I had dropped a large sum of diamonds into a woman's bag in order to get her to carry them across the border, would I be comfortable *not* keeping an eye on her?"

At that, Madeline froze. "I guess I wouldn't either."

Seeing interest from people around her, he quickly ducked into a coffee shop and moved her through and out the rear exit and into the back alley. He watched her process the information and the realization that she'd probably been targeted right from the beginning by other people than just the ones who she saw here in Paris.

When he pulled her out the other side of the coffee

shop, she looked around. "The least you could have done was stop and let me grab a coffee." That note of humor in her tone revealed that she'd gotten her equilibrium back again.

He smiled and nodded. "I just thought that maybe you would want to go someplace where we could sit and relax *while* we have that coffee."

"Wouldn't that be nice," she muttered, "and I am getting tired again." He frowned at that, and this time she was more aware of his stare. "Are you thinking that she did something to me?"

"I'm not sure, but it's been a couple days later now. Generally most drugs wouldn't have lasted that long in your system, but I don't know what else might have happened."

She glared at him. "Every time you bring up these things, it gives me the hives about ever traveling again."

He nodded. "Yet I think we're better off knowing the truth, don't you?"

"Not if the truth means the woman who sat beside me on purpose was to keep an eye on me and was also a part of my kidnapping afterward."

"I'm wondering now if the kidnapping was most likely just because they didn't know what had happened to the diamonds that Anna took. Chances are good that Anna was either on that same flight or in the airport waiting to collect your bag, and then took off. But, because you were held captive together, the smugglers will wonder if you didn't have something to say or to do with what Anna did as well."

"*Uh-oh.* The smugglers won't take a chance on that, right? Even if they have all the diamonds, they won't take a chance that maybe I was told something."

"They can't," he stated simply. "Too much money is at

stake for a regular smuggling operation with a system that has probably worked quite well for them for a long time. Nobody'll be too willing to give that up, although it is common in situations such as this to find new avenues anyway."

"You would think they would already have plans A, B, and C set up, just to evade the cops. However, we're now talking about evading one of their own," she muttered.

As they walked along, he pointed out a vehicle coming toward them. "That's Brody."

Sure enough, it pulled up at their side, and Brody barked, "Get in."

As they got in, she examined the vehicle. "What did you do, steal it?"

"Yes, I did."

She cringed at his admission. "They'll blame me for that too, won't they?"

He laughed. "No, and, if I don't cause any damage, it'll go back to its owner in the same condition. And the detective called. They found the security guard. Dead in a dumpster. Plus, Terk updated us on Garret. He's still tied up with the MI6 flag."

Madeline frowned and asked, "Who's Garret?"

Nate laughed and filled her in.

Brody added, "But I saved the good news for last. Langdon has an update on the missing diamond stash."

Nate smiled. "Good, but now we must figure out who best to share that info with."

Brody nodded. "As a barter? As a way out? Good idea. Let's hold on to that intel and save it for when we need it the most."

Meanwhile, Brody continued to drive, while Nate explained his gift of camouflage to Madeline, to help keep her safe, even if he wasn't with her. "A technique is involved," he began, "and it's all got to do with energy."

"God, that whole energy thing again," she muttered. "And to think all I ever did was spread good energy around to help people heal. … It never occurred to me that using the same energy could help me transform myself, effectively hiding in plain sight."

"In our job, the ability to blend in is almost as important as the energy to heal," he murmured.

"Of course."

"The healers in our group would completely disagree with us, and, if you did get hurt, we'll definitely have people ready to help you."

"Let's hope so," she muttered, "because this isn't exactly going the way any of us planned, is it?"

"Nope, it sure isn't." Nate sighed. "Now, we need you to figure out who the woman was with you on the plane."

"That's easy enough. Check the flight and see who was sitting there. Although"—she winced—"the woman did say she had already changed her flight once."

"That's okay. We can figure out who was supposed to be there, get a photo, and then go through the manifest of everybody on the flight that day," he explained. "That should give us something to go on."

"I hope so," she muttered, "but chances are we'll find another dead body at the end of it. Another *dead in a dumpster* body."

"Not if we can get there fast enough."

Brody drove them to the entrance of yet another hotel.

"How do you guys find your way around here? I feel as if I've been here just as long as you have, and yet I have no idea where I am."

"Navigation is a skill," Brody murmured. "One I happen to be particularly good at."

And again she realized he probably meant energy. "Glad to hear that," she noted. "It's much more appealing than stealing cars."

He chuckled, a laugh that was both wicked and contagious. "You never know what skills you can come up with in a pinch," he declared, with a smile. "And, right now, these skills benefit everybody, so I'm not apologizing."

"No, definitely don't do that." She waved her hand. "That would make way too much sense right now."

He smiled at her. "Just keep your sense of humor and don't question us if we seemingly bark orders at you. We're trying to keep you safe. We *will* get you out of this eventually."

She frowned. Even though everything had gone terribly wrong, and they were still trying to avoid so many things and escape from others, she had joined up with these two guys she believed in. To the best of Brody's ability, and possibly even if forced to take a bullet, he would do the best he could for her. She looked over at Nate and realized that she got the exact same reading coming from him as well.

For the first time in far too long, she relaxed.

As soon as they got settled into the new hotel, Nate sat next to Madeline and phoned the detective but had to leave a message, just saying it was urgent.

When the detective called back almost immediately, his tone was apologetic. "Sorry. I was on the other phone.

What's going on?"

Nate put the call on Speakerphone and had Madeline explain about the woman seated next to her on her flight to Paris.

"Shit, and yet you're right. It makes total sense. Why would they have let that amount of diamonds loose without having some backup close by."

"Exactly. What if Madeline had found the stash in her travel bag or had changed her flight plans?" Nate looked over at Madeline. "He'll need a description, as much as you can remember about that woman beside you."

She stared at him. "You know she was probably in disguise, right?"

"I'm sure she was," the detective stated, "but that doesn't matter. We still must get everything you've got in terms of information to give us."

She nodded. The detective was right. "I don't have very much."

"Doesn't matter. I need it. *All* of it."

She took a deep breath and slowly told him what she knew.

"Did she talk about anything, anybody?"

"She talked about her family, talked about wanting to give them a good life. I don't even know how we got onto that topic. At one point in time, she was teary-eyed." Getting there, she looked at Nate in horror, as something clicked inside her. "Do you think she was forced to do this too?" she asked him.

"Stop. These people are due no feelings, no sympathy. Conning people, using people, is what they do."

She glared at him. "If I can't feel empathy, I can't do my work," she muttered. "So, you've got to expect a certain amount."

"I can expect a certain amount," he noted cautiously, "but we also must keep in mind that this smuggling ring quite possibly involves dozens of people, and those dozens of people could all be out looking for you right now."

Madeline shook her head. "It only makes sense if they really think that I saw something."

"No," the detective snapped. "You may have *heard* something straight from Anna or this woman on the flight next to you, something about the missing diamonds, a second stash of them. The fact that Anna was incarcerated with you means the smugglers can't take a chance on what you may have been told or what Anna may have given you."

"She didn't tell me any smuggler's secrets or give me anything," Madeline wailed.

The detective interjected, "The smugglers don't know that. Don't forget that the word on the street is that a very tempting ransom is offered for finding the missing stash. ... You don't want to find out what lengths desperate people will go to when it comes to their greed."

Madeline went silent, as the color drained from her face.

The detective added, "I don't mean to scare you, unless it saves your life. So you need to be aware of the extreme danger you are in, right now, which will follow you wherever you go, until those other diamonds are found."

She nodded and swallowed, then let out a breath. "I get it," she muttered. "I didn't ask to be in this position."

"No, neither did we," Nate replied, "but this is what we have to deal with right now."

She went on to give the detective as much of a description as she could remember, slowly walking her way through the details. "She wasn't terribly friendly, but she kept up a running commentary that made the plane ride go very quickly," she admitted, "and, for that, I was grateful. I'm not a great traveler anyway." She turned to Nate. "Sorry, it's not as if you needed to be told that."

"You're doing just fine," he muttered.

"Okay, so that's the rough description," the detective noted. "Chances are, some disguise was in play, but this might give us something to go on."

"And Madeline's seat was changed. Tell him about that," Nate reminded Madeline.

"Yeah, I forgot. I was asked to take somebody else's seat."

"Tell him why," Nate urged her patiently.

"I was asked to move and to sit beside this woman because a couple on their honeymoon wanted to sit together," she explained, with a smile.

"You didn't think to mention this earlier?" the detective snapped.

"Of course not. That stuff happens all the time."

The detective sighed.

She imagined that he was rolling his eyes too. Of course it was all very important now. Given her kidnapping and learning about the smuggling ring, she should have known better.

Manshue added, "I'll send some names and photos through, once we work through this."

As soon as that phone call ended, Nate turned to her. "Seems you have met at least six of the smugglers."

Her eyes went wide.

Nate continued. "The first three—the supposed honeymoon couple and the extra woman—probably appeared at the beginning of your flight, so they could slip the diamonds into your bag and could keep an eye on you and your travel bag. Then, when your plane landed in France for that two-day layover, the first trio handed you off to another three-person team, probably your two kidnappers and Anna. The smugglers can't have just one person following you because you might notice the same guy always around you, but also because they have backup plans in play from the beginning. You understand that now, right?"

She shook her head. "I had no idea. I would never in my wildest dreams have thought this was even possible."

"That's why it has worked so well for them. They get you beside somebody, somebody who seems harmless, where they can keep an eye on you. Before you know it, they have used you as a mule to get their contraband through customs, and soon afterward they take your bag, and they're off to the races."

"And just stealing my bag would have been fine," she conceded. "I would have cheerfully handed over my bag if I knew *then* what I know now and what it would mean for my life."

"Of course you would have, but that's not how they operate. Anonymity is the preferred avenue for them, but, when that option is taken away, they're just trying to salvage the situation, without losing their stash."

"*Great*," she muttered. "So how safe are we here?"

"Safe enough for the moment."

She glared at him. "You know your wording is not helping, right?"

"Yet it's the truth. We now have a little bit more information, and we need to take it and run. So we're here, while everybody gets on with the research and hopefully finds the answers that we need," he added. "Meanwhile, you need to think about everybody you have seen since we've been together, and tell me if any of them looked even somewhat familiar."

She blinked. "I don't understand."

"Those six smugglers we have identified were all in disguise. So think about the people we pass on the street, think about the people that you met on the plane or met on the bus, think about … anybody who looks even somewhat familiar to you."

"First was an airport and then a bus station, so, of course, a bunch of people were there."

He looked at her grimly. "Which people?"

She pondered that. "I think the honeymoon couple for sure got off the plane and joined me on the bus. It's pretty standard for people exiting the plane to head for the various buses, but I'm not certain if more were on my particular bus."

"That could have been the handoff point, from team A to team B." He nodded, with a smile.

"But they already had my … No, they didn't have my bag," she corrected, sagging back into her chair. "They were still following me because I was clutching my bag, right?"

"Absolutely, and when team A couldn't just grab your bag out of your hands on the plane or even after landing, that's why they needed the extra handoff."

She nodded. "Again, I feel incredibly foolish."

"Don't. You were victimized, and these people were trying to steal your bag. So I wouldn't at all feel bad about that. You did succeed for the longest time, and these were pros, so almost nobody can evade them forever."

"Maybe," she muttered. "But still, it feels shitty."

He smiled. "The good news is now we should start getting answers and, with answers," he said, "will come a chance for you to put this behind you."

She smiled. "I hope so."

"Yeah, but still keep thinking about the people you've met up until now and everything that you've been telling us. We have to get everything else you've got stored in your brain, even if you haven't remembered it yet."

"I will certainly try. I'm just not sure how to go about it."

"To start with, did you see the woman on the plane again?" he asked. "She's the one you got the best look at."

"No, I didn't see her afterward, not even on the bus. … I saw Anna when I woke up in the hotel room, but I don't remember seeing her earlier at all."

"So, you don't remember seeing her anywhere else?"

"No, I don't." She shrugged. "I mean, honestly, I didn't expect to see anybody I knew."

"No, of course not," he said. "You were on your way to Africa."

"Which is even more belatedly irritating," she admitted. "I mean, all kinds of people were on those flights, so why me, why my bag?"

"Did you happen to …"

When he hesitated, she glared at him. "Did I happen to what?"

He half smiled. "I know this is not what you want to be asked, but did you happen to use your healing energy at any point in time while you were traveling?"

She frowned at him, dumbfounded. "You mean, on random people?"

"Or on yourself," he added, "because, the minute you open that healing energy, it's quite possible it would have attracted people to you."

She blinked. "As you know, I don't have any formal training in this energy work. So, if I would have used that energy, I would have just opened it up and used it." She raised both hands. "It's not as if I do any mantra or anything beforehand."

At that, Brody looked up at them both. He had been seated off to the side, working on his laptop. "You need to start protecting yourself," he stated. "Every time you open up your energy, you can bring in all kinds of other energy—energy that you don't want and certainly don't need. It doesn't even have to necessarily be people on this earthly plane."

At that, she blanched. "Good God, that is not something I want to think about."

"But you need to, and it's possible that other people can utilize that energy themselves." Brody was not pulling any punches.

"He's right," Nate confirmed. "And, if that's what's happened here, when you used your good energy to knock out your own headache, that may have attracted others to you because of that goodness."

She stared. "You know that's beyond ... wild, right?"

Brody nodded, but his face was serious. "It might be," he agreed, "but it's also how this life works, particularly when you deal with energy. You can learn to protect yourself by doing certain things. If you don't follow that protocol," he murmured, "shit happens."

CHAPTER 10

MADELINE SAT BACK, sagging into the hot and uncomfortable cheap hotel furniture, but that didn't even matter because she was way too stunned at his words as she struggled to even understand. She took a deep breath and then realized she had no idea how to respond. She was at a loss for words. "You're saying that I brought this on myself?" She looked over at Nate for confirmation.

He winced. "No, Brody's not really saying that. He's just trying to—"

"Yes, I am," Brody corrected, his tone hard. "That's exactly what I'm saying. People don't realize how dangerous this energy can be in the wrong hands. It's powerful, and other people can take advantage. I'm not saying you did it on purpose, and I get that some of this is new to you."

As he paused for a breath, she let out the one she'd been holding, slowing releasing it as she stared at him.

Brody continued. "You need to understand the potential ramifications." Then turning to face Nate, Brody added, "And you don't need to coddle her."

"I didn't know," Madeline muttered. "I didn't know any of that."

"I get that," Brody replied. "We come up against a lot of newbies with abilities who don't have the slightest idea about how to use them. I keep telling Terkel that he should set up a school or something to protect these people. He just looks at me in horror. Still, we need to figure this out because so few people out there have any training or any understanding of just how much danger they're opening themselves up for."

She just stared at him. "I had a headache. I was dehydrated," she began, "but I didn't have any water. I was in line to show my ticket to the stewardess. I didn't want to leave the line. They were boarding, and I just ran. While I was running, I used energy to keep up because I was tired and stressed. Honesty, I didn't think anything of it."

At that, Brody nodded. "No, you didn't, and I'm not surprised because you were so stressed from traveling. Yet it doesn't change the fact that, once you open that energy, other people can feel it. Whether they can utilize it or not doesn't matter as much as you opened that door and didn't protect yourself first," he stated, shaking his head. "It's a completely different thing once that door is opened."

"And, once that healing energy is freed, other people around you can heal too. Have you ever had that happen?" Nate asked, eyeing her closely now.

She nodded, understanding that a bit better. "When I would be in surgery," she began, shifting her gaze to the distance, through all the operations she'd been a part of, "I would do my regular nursing work, then would send healing energy for the patient. I would do everything I could to help them heal, but other people around me would start to feel better too. I noticed that, but I just figured it was a lucky side benefit for them."

Nate smiled. "And that's a good thing. Obviously we don't want you to stop using your healing energy. However, you must learn how to protect yourself from people who may have been attracted to that same energy, but for very different reasons. If they were looking for somebody to pick for this smuggling job, they would have been attracted to you. And you've been wondering, *Why you*, right?"

"Yes," she whispered. "And that is exactly why I don't want to travel anymore."

Brody nodded. "And yet, if you go to Terkel's place, you may have to."

She stared at him, aghast. "Why?"

"Because we work as a team," Brody shared. "I get that you wouldn't want to travel again anytime too soon, given what's happened recently, but that doesn't mean there won't be times when a second team might have to travel to help the first team."

"If it meant saving somebody, of course," she replied instantly. "Particularly if I wasn't traveling alone. The *alone part* was fairly distressing."

"Yet you were happy to go originally?"

"Sure, I was up for the adventure, but the adventure paled very quickly," she muttered, and then she glared at them both. "I get it. You guys travel all the time, but for me? … It wasn't quite the same."

"Traveling alone as a single female isn't easy for a lot of women. And, with the energy that you were utilizing, I'm sure you had an awful lot of people talking to you, draining you in ways that you probably weren't even aware of," Brody added.

Madeline frowned. "Definitely a lot of people were talking to me," she agreed, "and I didn't know why. Maybe that's what traveling was all about for anybody, but it wore me down. I'm social in certain circumstances, but then I need some time alone again to recharge my energy."

"Yeah, the psychologists have terms for that." Nate gave

her half a smile. "I'm not exactly an extrovert myself, but it's easy to talk to you. And, if it's easy for *me* to talk to you, then it'll really be easy for other people."

She stared at him. "But you are both very open and easy to get along with."

Brody considered her for a moment, then turned to Nate. "Did she just say that we're *both very open and easy to get along with?*"

Nate grinned. "Yeah, she did. That's exactly what she said."

Then they both exploded into unfettered laughter.

She looked from one to the other. "I don't get it. Why are you both laughing?"

"Because we're both the opposite of that," Brody declared, with a huff.

"I'm not exactly an open and easygoing person. That much I can say for sure," Nate muttered. "I don't really care for people much, and I would just as soon most of them walk off a cliff," he muttered out loud. "The fact that you would even think of me as friendly is a bit of a shock. I've worked hard to make myself come across as the opposite."

She stared at him, then looked from one to the other and smiled. "Now I know that you're just egging me on," she declared, "because absolutely no way would I believe that. You guys are both open, friendly, and super easy to talk to."

Brody stared at her in an assessing way. "You may have a certain energy that makes people open up and talkative, and *that*," he said, raising an eyebrow, "is a very interesting aspect to your energy."

"It could be just part of my counseling certification I'm working on too. Why does this interest you?" she asked suspiciously. "You're already thinking how that can help your team, aren't you?"

Brody chuckled. "Of course. That energy skill is not a bad idea and a good one to add to our team," he shared. "No doubt that we could use help at times to make a certain environment more open and relaxing, easing people into conversations. That could help a lot. Also I find it personally fascinating. Terk will too. Honestly, I'm *not* talkative normally, not until I get to know people. And, just for the record, I'm *not* friendly," he snapped, glaring at her. She burst out laughing, while he just stared. "I don't get it," he said, looking over at Nate. "Does your energy work make people talkative for you?"

"Nope, and I already tried it a couple times," he admitted, grinning. "It's her. It's definitely her."

She shrugged. "I think you guys are crazy."

"No, we're not," Brody argued, "but it would be interesting to bring you back to Terkel's."

"Yeah, but I don't know that I'm even welcome," she reminded him.

"After all this, and the things that we can tell Terkel, sure you are." Brody considered her. "And I don't know anything about your healing ability, and we do have healers on the team already. Yet, as far as they're concerned, we never have enough of them."

"Sure," she muttered, as she looked over at Nate. "What is your ability?" She looked from one to the other. "Or do you both just use your energy to hide and to do things?"

Nate answered that question. "Energy work can be all kinds of things," he began. "As energy workers, we can learn to do more, but I find that each of us has our own special skill set. I do use my energy to hide, yes, which is why nobody has seen us outside *yet*," he shared, as he looked directly at her. "That is also why we have to stay one step ahead of the bad guys. And Brody, he acts as an early warning system, not to mention a navigation specialist, among other abilities."

She blinked. "Do these abilities always work for you?"

"No." Brody shook his head. "That is something I'm working on. In fact, Terk's whole team is working on this. Sometimes energy works better than other times. We do know that, if we are underground or surrounded by two-feet-thick concrete, those physical conditions will impair our abilities. Of course, as you found out firsthand, being drugged interrupts our energy work for sure."

"Wow. That's absolutely fascinating. Yet you don't tell people about your abilities, do you?" she asked, now looking at Nate.

"No, we sure don't," they both answered simultaneously.

She glanced from one to the other.

"Just like *you* didn't share with us that you are an energy worker," Brody pointed out. "We only trust other energy workers on the side of good. Plus, we don't want to talk to people regardless."

Madeline laughed. "Right, so we're back to that part about you *not* being friendly."

"Exactly," Brody replied. "I'm not. Yet around your special *fairy dust*, it seems I am. But"—he pointed a finger at her—"stop that shit. We need a certain hard edge to us to do this job properly. We were basically three strangers thrown together here, living atop one another, so there are boundaries even between energy workers who are friends, where our own freedoms are not infringed, where permission is needed before using that energy on someone. Now at home, show your healing aura all you want and let it draw people in."

She flushed bright red and opened her mouth.

Brody interrupted her. "Don't apologize again. And don't go into worry mode or into feeling guilty or responsible either. You're a newbie. We were all green to begin with. After all, there is no energy worker school, even though, as I said earlier, we keep asking Terk to set one up. You learn by watching us, by hearing us hand down whatever wisdom we've got to share. We know that you'll learn more about this and grow with each lesson. No judgment here. We are in a judgment-free zone when it comes to our team of energy workers because we all accept each other and haven't found that acceptance anywhere else. So just keep learning. You'll be fine."

Nate added, while squeezing her hand, "What he said."

Tears filled her eyes, but she smiled and nodded at Brody. "Thank you," she whispered.

Nate pointed to Brody. "They paired me with Brody because we seem to be of the same temperament, I suppose. I'm not really a people guy either," he admitted, eyeing her curiously. "Brody and I are a matching set."

"Yet you guys have been super sweet to me."

Brody just looked at her, then at Nate, while shaking his head. "Wow, if she ever gets around the women at home, telling them how *super sweet* I am, they will all wonder what happened to me."

"If you say so. But you are right about one thing. I guess I do make people comfortable enough to talk to me," Madeline said. "Something about me puts people at ease because they do talk a lot to me. Yet, if you ask me, it's irritating sometimes."

Brody nodded. "Sounds like hell to me."

Again she chuckled. When Brody glared at her, she smiled even brighter. "See? I get that your glare works for you to keep people away. Really, it's just a tool that you use to keep them at a distance. I could probably do that to keep people away, but I don't really see the point because it backfires and makes everyone chattier."

"What do you mean exactly?" Nate asked.

"Because they talk to me anyway, even when I use energy to stop them."

Nate frowned and held up a hand. "Let me just ask you something here. If you and I head into a relationship," Nate asked, with a half-horrified expression, "are you telling me that our life will be full of people tripping over each other to talk to you?"

Brody laughed and laughed and laughed. "Oh, man, because of your camouflage, … we haven't seen her out in public yet, have we?"

"No, we haven't. Not sure I want to know either," Nate grumbled.

"But what am I supposed to do?" Madeline asked. "People are friendly—at least to me," she added, glaring at both men. "Besides, every time I'm with each of you, you end up being friendly too."

Nate sighed. "Yeah, you may be rubbing off on us." He looked over at Brody, who seemed clearly horrified.

"She better not be," Brody muttered. "I don't need that. No way in hell I want that fairy dust to stick to me."

Just then Terkel called Nate.

Nate answered, "Did you hear all that?"

"Yes, I did," Terk confirmed, his tone curious. "I've never heard of that ability."

"No? I haven't either, and we don't know how effective

it is. But, in the airport, then on the plane, even the bus, I'm sure everybody was drawn to her. Making her an easy target."

"That's something she'll have to learn to minimize, especially when she's out in public."

Nate pointed out, "She may already intend to minimize it, in the sense that she's much more aware of it and prepared for all the dangers that can and have happened so far. Still, she's untrained so …"

"We'll confirm all that when she gets here, so she gets the right training."

Nate looked over at Madeline and repeated that for her benefit. "Terkel says, when you get back to his place, he can work on your training."

She looked at Nate in delight and then reached for the phone. "Terkel?"

"Hello, Madeline. I am glad we crossed paths. Interesting skills, by the way."

"I don't know how effective they are, though," she replied, suddenly worried. "I mean, I don't really have much of a chance to use them."

"No, but you were heading over to work on Bullard's patients, right?"

"Yes. I'm a nurse, and I'm getting a counseling certificate. So I always try to help heal people, and that job just appealed."

"Yet not now?" he asked curiously.

"No, not so much about the job itself but the travel to get there. As a matter of fact, I was just telling the guys I don't really want to travel at all, not after this kidnapping event."

"Sometimes you might have to. All of us have to, at

some point."

"So Brody was telling me, in some detail. It seems he's got a word on nearly every subject. Nate can hardly get a word in."

A moment of silence came on the other end, "Did you say Brody talks a lot?"

"Yeah, he's really very friendly, both of them are," she stated warmly. "I really want to thank you for sending them over to help. I was very frightened, and they've both been so kind and really put me at ease."

At that, Terkel started to laugh, giggling like a girl even. After that he collapsed into a fit of coughing and finally got a hold of himself. "Now I really have to meet you in person," he stated. "because Brody is *not* friendly. Brody is my crankiest team member. He remains distant, silent, and hard to open up even with his other team members, and frankly he's got some pretty stiff competition."

"No, honestly, he's a sweetheart," Madeline repeated. Brody scowled at her. "Although he's looking at me with a shocked expression right now, as if he really doesn't appreciate what I'm saying. Is he really that hard to get along with?"

"Yes, normally he is," Terkel stated, with laughter still in his tone. "Pass the phone over to him, would you?"

Smiling, she handed the phone to Brody. "He wants to talk to you."

He snatched the phone from her hand and continued to glare at her.

"He's glaring at me again," she said to Terkel. Then she beamed and smiled his way, and the frown disappeared from his face. "Oh wait, he's being friendly now too."

Brody just realized what she did. "That's not fair."

She shrugged. "I don't want people frowning. It makes

me nervous."

Brody raised his free hand. "Terkel, she's driving me nuts."

"Sounds as if it's a hell of a combination." Terk's voice filled the room, even though Brody held the phone. "How's Nate handling it?"

"He's smitten," Brody shared instantly. "Severely smitten." And shot Nate an evil grin.

Terkel started to laugh again, barely able to talk. "That makes perfect sense."

Nate glared over at Brody. "No, it doesn't," he snapped. "And smitten is one thing. That's not what we're talking about."

"No, it isn't," Terkel answered, his voice warm and full of humor. "But the bottom line is, her spreading her energy around does explain why she was chosen as a mule to begin with and why we have so many people all over her. Plus, her constant need for sleep and food? ... She's draining her energy reserves several times a day. And yet all that output is why nobody has hurt her so far. Well, that and Nate's camouflage."

"Oh." Nate turned to look at her. "I hadn't considered it in that light."

"That may prove to be her saving grace."

"Maybe, but only if she can talk to them," he noted. "It's tricky really because I hadn't even noticed that she was getting us to talk." He shook his head. "That explains another of my worries too, how she's often out of breath."

"That could very well be because of her energy expenditures," Terk noted.

"We did figure out what happened on the plane."

"I heard part of the conversation," Terk muttered. "Fill

me in on the rest of the details."

And, with that, they got down to the business of sharing the rest with him.

Brody ended it with, "We are still waiting for the detective."

"That's the other reason I'm calling. I'm sending a lot of photos to your laptop. If you want to bring it up now, we can go over them and see if she recognizes anybody." With that, they quickly opened up the laptop and brought up the emails.

She looked at the faces and instantly swore. "That's the woman sitting beside me on the plane."

"Good," Terk said. "Tell me what picture number you just ID'd."

When she told Terk, Nate then asked her, "Anybody else?"

She quickly identified the man who she had changed seats with, giving Terk the ID number for that photo. "Are they all involved?"

Terk replied, "Yes, they are, and did you see the other man in this same photo?"

Another male was in the photo. "No, I don't recognize him."

"He works at the airline, and he's a known associate of the smuggling ring."

"*Great*, so they had people on the inside at the hotel and at the airport as well?"

"Yeah. How about the next photo?"

She looked at that guy in the snapshot and frowned. "Now, remember that I was drugged for two full days. Yet I feel as if he delivered something to us, so room service maybe?"

"Good call," Terk replied. "That's one of the hotel security guys who also delivered room service in that hotel. He was connected to Anna, as they went to school together."

"Wow. … So you were right," Madeline said. "Anna was involved."

"It looks like it, but that doesn't mean she wanted to stay involved."

"Right, and yet her bid for freedom came at a very high price."

"She may have felt as if she had no choice," Nate suggested. "So let's not judge her for her actions at this point. All I want to do is get you out of here safely."

"The cops won't let me leave," she snapped. "And that really bothers me."

"Why does it bother you? Because you couldn't sweet talk the detective into letting you leave?" Terk asked curiously.

"Oh my gosh," she gasped, searching for a reason, and it was evident all over her face. "Every time we've seen him or even spoken to him, … I've gotten so angry and upset that I didn't even think about it."

"You should try a different approach," Terkel offered, "and maybe we can get you home that much sooner. I think that would be a grand idea."

"Yeah, you and me both," she muttered. "I'm coming empty-handed though, except for what clothes Nate picked up for me."

"That's fine," Terk replied. "We have stores over here too."

She winced at that. "Once again here I go saying something completely stupid."

"Not at all," he declared graciously. "As soon as you get

here, we will all be very interested in meeting you."

"I'm not very good at dog-and-pony shows."

"Good, neither are we." And, with that, Terkel disconnected.

She looked over at Brody and Nate. "Is he always that friendly?" But Nate had a smile on the corner of his lips, while Brody stared at her, shaking his head.

"No, he sure isn't," Brody snapped, "but apparently there is just something about you. I am amazed that he talked to you this much. He usually hangs up before I'm done with my report."

She shrugged. "I'm used to that from people. It's generally a nice world out there, and, most of the time, everyone has been very friendly and open. It's just that, when I'm tired, I want the world to go away."

"Yeah, I'm that way all the time," Brody muttered.

She gave him a beaming smile. "Yet you've been nothing but a sweetheart to me."

He shook his head, got up, then walked over to the kitchen, where they had a little bit of food they had dragged along from the last place.

"A real meal might be nice at some point," she suggested.

"We can get a real meal," Brody replied. "I'm going out and doing some reconnaissance anyway. Research is happening with our team and the detective's. So, now what we need is for the bad guys to be picked up."

"Do you think that's possible?" she asked.

"Sure, it's possible," he asked. "What do you think we're doing?"

She flushed. "Honestly, I wasn't sure."

He rolled his eyes. "I guess we deserve that, considering

all we've done is haul you from one place to another."

"And yet you've kept me safe, so whether anybody has been tracking us, I don't know how. But, hey, … *uh-oh.*" Then she stopped. "You know what would really be bad? … If they had a cop on their staff."

"You mean as part of their smuggling team?" Nate asked to clarify.

Brody noted, "It's pretty common to have law enforcement of some kind in on it, but it doesn't mean that all cops are bad."

"Of course not," she said, "but our detective should be checking any known associates."

"Sure, and they are. So, it's a case of sit and wait again."

"That is getting very hard to do," she muttered. "Are you sure we can't go out to eat or for coffee? Something?"

Nate hesitated, then looked over at Brody. "Is she using up energy like I think she is?"

Brody nodded, crossing his arms over his chest. "Don't use your charming ways on us," he stated, his tone hard. "Particularly not right now, when our resolve and clear thinking is all that's keeping you safe. The minute you go out there, we can't do that."

She sagged back and nodded. "Sorry, I was just hoping that maybe I could get out of here, get a bit of shopping done, and think about something else for a change."

"No," Brody replied. "Save that for when it's over."

Curled up in the corner of the couch, frustrated with the entire waiting process, she was almost fuming with fury. All she wanted to do was tell the police to eff off and then get herself back to England. With a big sigh, she realized she certainly had plenty of time now to consider that whole *friendly people* thing. She could specifically look back at several points in her life when she had attempted to make people be nicer to her.

Not out of spite, but more because she'd been afraid. At seventeen, a group of young men at school had tormented her incessantly. She had prayed for relief every night, hoping that something would change, and, over a period of about two months, it had changed, and they were much nicer to her after that.

She later found something online about spirit talking, and, realizing she had absolutely nothing to lose, she dove into it and had an interesting result. School had ended not too long after that. Much later, once she was in nursing school, she'd had a professor who seemed to single her out for the worst things possible. She knew that she somehow had become a target on his radar, and he just wouldn't let up. So she'd done the same thing and had incorporated the same spirit talking to him, night after night. It seemed to work. He softened his attitude and ended up being quite a bit nicer over time. Everybody around her made comments about it, and she had just laughed it off, saying that he'd just finally gotten to know her. But now she wondered.

She had wondered a lot at the time, and afterward she'd realized that, with her world in such a mess, she had finally found something to help. This seemed to be something she could do to make her life a little easier.

It's not that she spoke to individual people on a spirit level every night, but she did repeat a series of affirmations that people would always treat her well, would always be friendly to her, would open up and talk to her, instead of giving her the cold shoulder. That had been added after a particular boyfriend wasn't open to her at all, and their relationship didn't progress because he just wouldn't talk.

Their relationship ended when he walked out of her life, before anything she tried to do to improve it had taken effect.

She'd always wondered if that relationship could have succeeded if she'd learned to do this earlier. Only as she realized the difference she was making in the operating room, did she consider that the two things were related. By then it was just a habit. When she looked at people, she smiled and sent them a blast of bright, cheerful energy. When people talked to her, and they were happy, of course she gave that same happiness back.

She wasn't doing anything to influence people, but … At that thought she stopped, closed her eyes, and pinched the bridge of her nose. Of course she was, but she was doing it in a good way for a good reason. She wanted the world to be a happier place, a nicer place. So, if doing this made a difference, how could anyone even argue against it? Of course there was no argument because she had no known correlation until her nursing in the surgery room took effect. Now, smack in the middle of the clutches of a smuggling ring, she couldn't ignore the cause and effect.

She had quite a comfortable relationship with both Brody and Nate, and she had to wonder if this relationship with Nate was also because of her *influence*. If so, was their relationship even real? That scared her, even shamed her, and made her more than a little afraid of what she was doing. She was freaking out about it now.

When Nate walked over and sat down beside her, his gaze was intent. He put his arm around her shoulders and whispered, "I don't see energy the same as a lot of gifted people, but it's hard to miss the fact that you're really troubled right now."

Sitting up, she hooked her arms around her knees. "What if this, … this good feeling between us is because of my energy? Because of what I send out there?"

He looked at her in surprise. "You mean, the fact that we care for each other?" he asked gently.

She flushed. "Yeah, that too," she muttered.

"Have you used that energy in order to have a relationship with somebody before?"

She shook her head, now aghast. "No, of course not. That would be morally wrong, not to mention creepy. Besides, with that kind of a deal, how can I trust that somebody would actually care about me? And please keep in mind there's a fine line between using the energy to help someone heal, lighten depression, ease a headache type of thing versus using it to control their actions and emotions."

"So why are you questioning it now?"

She flushed again and stared at him. "I don't know. I guess because I hadn't really considered my actions as being wrong before. Yet, when you put it the way you just did, it seems horrific. So now I'm wondering if what we have between us is even real." When his lips twitched, she glared at him. "No laughing at me," she muttered. "This is very deep soul-searching stuff."

He agreed. "It absolutely is, and those of us who have energy, who can work energy, have a greater responsibility to confirm that everything is done in a moral and ethical way."

She agreed wholeheartedly with that. "So, how do we tell?" she repeated.

He reached out his hand and placed it palm up. "Put your hand in mine." Hesitantly, she unlocked her clasped hands and placed one on his. An immediate zing of energy came on so strong that she pulled back her hand. She stared at him in shock. "What the hell was that?"

He chuckled. "That was energy, just good old-fashioned energy. Now," he added, trying to calm her down, "it's nothing to worry about, but I am amped up, and the power we share is enhanced ever-so-slightly, just so you couldn't doubt it, just so you have a distinctive chance to recognize this reaction as the expected energy shared between us."

"But, if you intentionally increased it on your end, then any other energy worker could have the same energy pop up between us if our hands touch. For that matter, I could eventually learn to increase my energy too, right?"

"Think of it this way. That is *my* energy, yes, but it's my energy reacting to your energy when our hands meet," he clarified. "If Brody put his hand in mine, I would not get the same response." From the other side of the room, Brody snorted, making Nate chuckle.

Brody declared, "Sure as hell better not be, man, or my wife would be really upset."

Nate smiled at Madeline, as he continued. "If you took Brody's hand, you wouldn't get the same response either."

Brody nodded at her, and she finally smiled. "So, what you're saying is, … this is because of the combination of our two energies and can't be replicated with just anybody else. Correct?"

"Exactly, the same as Brody and his wife would have a similar reaction because it would be tuned in to the shared energy of their souls," Nate explained. "Our energy, when blended together, gives a very unique signature, whereby anybody could identify that energy specifically, but, for us, it feels like home. It feels right."

She slowly nodded at that but still frowned. "But what if my energy to make you talk and to be friendlier … was affecting that reaction when we join hands, so that you're looking at me in a completely different way?"

He chuckled. "When we first met, you were so panicked and so upset that I automatically used my energy to comfort you and to calm you down. So, you could say that my energy did the exact same thing to you."

She stared at him and then asked again, this time in a miserable tone, "So how do we know that what we have is real?"

He reached out his other hand, placing it on hers. "At some point in time you'll have to trust that the energy you feel, that the energy you can assess in your own heart is real. Do you ever doubt when something's real?" he asked curiously.

"No, I usually know pretty well when it is," she stated, "but I've never come up against anything like this before. So, a part of me is wondering how it could possibly be real. I don't know who you are. I don't know anything about you."

"Ah, but you do," he corrected, "and you already know everything that matters. You were born with a set of morals and ethics. You can see that in other people, even without your energy skills."

She blinked at that. "I guess," she agreed slowly. "I hadn't considered it that way."

"Still, you must go by feelings, by energy, and by how your heart feels," he added. "And, by all means, if you don't want anything to do with me, say so right now," he stated. "I'm not trying to push you into anything. I didn't expect to care at all. I've been on lots of jobs with brilliant women, and I've never once had this reaction."

She looked at him hopefully. "Seriously?"

"Never," he declared. "I would be a very busy man if I

suddenly became some Don Juan with every woman I met."

Brody snorted again.

Nate pointed out, "Remember too that I have my own set of ethics and morals, which doesn't allow for me to play with women's emotions."

Madeline nodded at Nate, but then glared at Brody. "You could give us some privacy."

"Yeah, I could, but, in case you haven't noticed, it's a pretty small place."

She sighed, then looked over at Nate. "He's right. I guess we didn't have to have this conversation right now."

"I'm not ashamed of it," Nate noted. "I'm guessing Brody went through his share of torment with his own partner. This is the stage of life we're at, and believe me that, if we both end up at Terkel's house, or castle," he corrected, with an eye roll, "I can't imagine that privacy will be all that easy to find there either. Terk's team is full of energy workers, who then married more energy workers. And a lot of them happen to be pregnant," he reminded Madeline, with a glance back at Brody, catching his wince. "The energy at the castle will change greatly from where it is at today to what it'll be in one year, when they have eight-plus energy-working babies and toddlers running around the place. So keep that in mind too."

She gasped. "That many?" she asked faintly.

"Yeah, and counting, as it seems that sharing living quarters with energy workers enhances all their gifts and makes them procreate immediately. And, in case you were wondering, even birth control doesn't seem to curtail this side effect of being an energy worker. So, if that worries you at all, I understand that."

Brody added, "You do have to put a few safeguards in

place, as to protection of the privacy of your thoughts and to the procreation decision—something that none of us really considered quickly enough."

She started to giggle but caught Brody's glare, yet saw the pride in his eyes. "You're gloriously happy, aren't you?"

He gave her a sheepish grin. "I didn't expect to be, but love?" He shrugged. "It changes you, and I never thought I would see love and children in my lifetime, not with this work and how people treat those of us with these skills. Yet here we are."

"I think it's wonderful," she replied, with a quiet joy for him. "I've been in the operating room with too many little kids on the table, who were suffering from all kinds of issues, some of them brought on by their parents, either physically or genetically. Not everybody should be a parent, and yet I think those who really want to be should be given that chance," she shared, still smiling at him. "I know you'll be a wonderful dad." Such warm confidence filled her tone that Brody eyed her suspiciously. She frowned and asked him, "What?"

"Well," he muttered, "you're a little too good at your energy gift, making me more open and friendly."

She burst out laughing. "By just complimenting you?"

"Yeah," he stated, glaring at her. "It's a sad world where not that many people hand out compliments."

"Oh, I know," she agreed, "and I think that's a great sadness of our times. We're all quick to criticize and very belated to give credit where credit is due. Yet you have come a long way in the last little while, and I think that is terrific."

He stared at her suspiciously. "How do you know I've come a long way?"

"I can see it in your energy," she shared. "Also in this

growth bar beside you, where your personal growth bar shows a tremendous increase."

At that, Brody's phone rang, and he put it on Speaker. "Terkel, what's up?"

"Did she just say what I thought she said?" Terk asked.

He burst out laughing. "Yeah, so now we're into discussions on personal improvement ratings," he stated, with an eye roll. "This lady is dangerous."

"Sounds as if she's much more of a counselor than I thought," Terk replied, his tone contemplative.

"Oh, God," Brody snapped, "we don't need that at home. Can you imagine what any standard psychologist or psychiatrist would do with a group of energy workers? Terk, you need to rethink this whole *inviting her* thing," he added, glaring at her, recoiling, as if she were a viper.

She chuckled. "Brody's uncomfortable with compliments," she explained to Terkel, yelling across the room. "It's okay though because he'll get better at it. I can help him with it."

Terkel started to laugh and laugh.

Brody just glared at her all the more. "None of that is allowed. I've already got my team and Terk in my head. I sure don't want you messing with it too."

She shook her head. "Did I mess with your head before? Have I messed with your head at all? No, I most certainly have not. I shared some nice, bright, loving energy, and that's just what a good person does. Plus, I'm a healer. So that's just what a healer would do as well. ... Now don't go telling me that I'm not a good person either. That will just make me angry."

"And then what?" he asked in a mocking tone. "You're a butterfly. How can a butterfly hurt anything when it's angry?"

"You don't want to test that," she stated. "It upsets me very much when I have to hurt somebody."

At that, Terkel asked her curiously. "Can you?"

She stopped, then eyed Nate and Brody before responding. "Everybody can to some degree. … I just reverse what I usually do, but I don't want to. It hurts me," she admitted, shuddering at the thought of it. "So why would I want to hurt myself?"

Brody got up, slowly walked over to her, and sat down. He took in her and Nate's joined hands and appeared to send some calming energy her way, to add to Nate's and her own. "When you say that you can reverse that process, what do you mean?"

She sighed. "In any spirit talk or energy work, you can send good energy or bad energy." She shivered. "You guys all know that, or you should anyway. I'm the newbie here, so I don't understand what the problem is, which is inherent in your question."

"No, of course not," Brody replied. "So let me put it this way. If you, even as a newbie, know you can send out good or bad energy, then why didn't you use some against your kidnappers?"

"For one," she began, "I don't remember anything about getting kidnapped. I was given drugs, for two days it seems, so I wasn't even conscious for the first forty-eight hours or thereabouts of my kidnapping event. Then, when the unmasked man came in our hotel room, finding Anna and me both tied up, he didn't do anything to hurt me or her. He was the only one I saw during my captivity, other than Anna. I decided to wait for answers from him, but I didn't get any. I did hope he would return and at least tell me what they wanted from me. I didn't expect much from Anna, as she was so shocked and upset that I was just trying to calm her down. Then, within a couple hours, the housekeeper arrived, and we escaped."

"Did you use any of that encouraging spirit talk with your kidnapper, trying to get him to open up to you?"

"In a way, yes," she replied. "I really didn't want him to hurt me, so I was sending calming energy mostly to him. I wasn't encouraging him to talk at that point. I suppose, if he had hurt me, I might have acted differently, but I don't know that for sure."

Terkel started to laugh. "So, let me get this straight. If you can do all that, why the hell are we protecting you?" he asked, with a chuckle. "Did you guys ever consider that maybe we should be protecting the other guys?"

She bolted to her feet. "That's not fair. I'm just trying to be a nice person."

"Yeah, but in our world," Terkel noted, his amusement still rippling through his tone, "not very many people are trying to be nice to us."

"I am," she declared. "It makes me a much better person. Plus, I can do a lot more with the energy and heal a lot more people when I am nice to others."

"And when you're not?"

"The personal interactions or the healing don't work so well," she muttered. "When I was forced to work in the ER, before I realized what I was doing, if I got angry at the doctors, it seemed to affect the surgical outcome." She sent an apologetic look to Brody and Nate. "Some doctors aren't very nice, and sometimes it takes them a while to become nice because they're stubborn and think they are perfect," she muttered. "I realized that when I got angry or upset, the healing wasn't as effective, and then the patient didn't do as well." She took a deep breath. "A child died on the table, and I felt so guilty, afraid I had caused the end result because I hadn't been able to send out healing energy, not as I would normally do. Even to this day I don't know if I'm to blame."

"And yet it's not your responsibility. Even the best doctors in the world still lose patients on the table," Nate replied. "No matter how good you may be, you can't heal the whole world."

"True," she conceded, "but I really want to heal the part of the world that I come into contact with."

NATE HAD NEVER heard anybody talk like Madeline before, and it seemed as if he was only now starting to get to know who she was on the inside. The thing was, everything he was learning just made him like her all that much more. He looked over at Brody to see a look of complete and utter surprise on his face. Nate grinned. "Even Brody doesn't quite know what to say."

She smirked at Brody. "As long as whatever comes out of his mouth is nice, it's fine," she shared, and then she chuckled. "But I know that it will be because that's the way I operate."

"Okay," Nate began, getting them back to the case at hand, "so nobody in the smuggling ring hurt you. But we still haven't rounded up all the ring members nor found their missing diamonds, and we need to, so you can put this nightmare behind you."

"Yes," she agreed, "but I'm still not happy that someone killed Anna. She didn't deserve that, and, while I don't know what her involvement was, I don't particularly care if she was involved. I know that she was absolutely terrified in that hotel room, and that has stuck with me."

"And when you gave her some of your energy to make her not so terrified, do you think that emboldened her to take action?" Nate watched her eyes grow wide, and then fear entered her gaze. He immediately squeezed her hand. "And again, it's not your fault."

"If I made her feel better and gave her that sense of confidence, so she could do something that got herself killed, then that is on me," she cried out.

"No, it's not," Nate declared. "Many more steps taken by other people led to that moment when you entered her life. Anna would not have been in that hotel room with you if she hadn't gotten herself there a long time ago. You cannot take on the responsibility for everybody in the world."

She let out several slow, deep breaths, as if trying to calm herself down on the inside, and she finally nodded. "I guess it's possible that she might have done that on her own. I didn't give her that much of my energy, as I was dealing with my own fears. We weren't together all that long, not when both of us were awake anyway. So, when we had a chance to leave when the cleaning lady came, we did. Next thing I knew, we were out of the room. When Anna ran, she ran flat-out. She wasn't looking to take me with her, or to stay with me to talk to the local police."

"No, that wouldn't have fit her escape plan either," Nate noted. "Remember that she had to get away from the smuggling ring, that she was probably intent on double-crossing them. Unfortunately for her it didn't work out the way she expected it to, and she ended up in the morgue. ... We sure don't want you to end up there. However, the diamond smugglers are short one stash. They probably know one shipment of the diamonds was found on Anna, and now the local authorities have those. Yet a second stash of diamonds is unaccounted for, and we don't want the smugglers to think that you have them. Whether they think you handed them over to the police or whatever, we have to convince them the diamonds are out of their reach."

"We asked the detective about putting out an announcement on that, right?"

Nate nodded. "The problem with doing that is, the cops are still trying to find other members of this ring, so confessing that they found one stash and are looking for the other just alerts the smugglers that we are on to them."

"Right, so the cops don't necessarily want to do something that would help clear me of this. So am I the bait for the smuggling ring?" She gasped at the thought.

"That's a discombobulated way of putting it, but I'm afraid so, yes," Nate replied, with Brody nodding his agreement, "and that's important for you to keep in mind."

"Sure," she muttered. "Yet, I just want to go home."

"Do you have a home? You keep saying *home*," Nate pointed out, eyeing her carefully. "Do you have an apartment or something? Do you have a place to go back to?"

"No. I stay with a girlfriend when I'm in between flat-sitting, so anything I really wanted to keep went to a storage unit," she shared, wincing at her own admission. "Then when the Africa job offer came, I donated all my clothes, except what would fit in my backpack, figuring that my wardrobe was for the wrong climate anyway. I got really good at keeping things simple," she noted. "I even gave up my storage unit too, so I'm pretty well footloose and fancy-free, as they say. You know those people who claim they can fit all their possessions in one car? Well, I can do it in a backpack."

"So that's why you've been antsy for clothes."

"I've become used to having only four, five, maybe six outfits to mix and match. My plan was that, when I got to Africa, I would go shopping for clothes appropriate for that climate. So, when I say, *I want to go home*, I just mean I want to get back to England."

"Got it."

When his phone rang a few minutes later, he pulled it out, half expecting to see Terkel's name on the screen, but it was the detective. "Hello, Manshue. Any progress?"

"We have in custody some of the members of the smuggling ring," he announced, his voice booming through the phone.

Nate quickly put it on Speaker, so that Brody could hear as well.

"Most of them have records, and two of them are currently wanted by Interpol," he shared in exasperation. "We cast out a wide net to see if we could get this wrapped up, could collect most of the ring. Madeline is officially off our suspect list, but I still highly recommend that you don't move at all, not until we can get this plan fully executed, including finding that other diamond stash."

"What about putting out some announcement about the diamonds being turned in to the authorities, so that the smugglers don't come after her again?"

"I did speak to the captain about that idea, but he wants us to hold off until we round up more of this group. The boss and others are setting up a sting right now, and, according to the online messages we're tracking, some international meeting has been called, and we're trying to get a team in place to make that happen."

"And of course you don't need our help."

"No, not only don't I need it, I can't have it," he declared. "Definitely not good for our relationships with other legal jurisdictions."

"Fine," Nate replied, "but our concern is keeping her safe and preferably getting her home."

"Until we pick up these guys and the missing diamonds, sit tight, and we'll get back to you." With that he disconnected.

She groaned, looking over at Nate. "I get that's what they want to happen, but it's really not good for me."

"Yet it's not bad for you either. If they can pick up the bulk of the smuggling ring and then find the missing diamonds, you'll be in the clear."

She smiled, with a sense of satisfaction. "Okay, I can do that." She looked around the room. "But I would really like some food and some more clothes, so I don't have to wash one outfit every night and hope it dries in time for the morning."

"Wow, Nate," Brody teased, walking back over to the table and the laptop there. "She can get pretty demanding, *huh?*"

Nate laughed. "Yeah, I'm sure she can, but, for now, her demands are within reason."

"They were *always* within reason," she stated in exasperation. "Asking for clothes is hardly asking for much."

"You have clothes on," Brody pointed out. "You probably have as much as we do."

She frowned at him and nodded. "I guess you guys travel light, don't you?"

"Absolutely. Now, food on the other hand," he said,

rubbing his stomach, "is another story. I could definitely use some of that, though I don't want to draw attention to us with too much room service."

"So, you'll head out?" she asked Brody.

"I'll head out," he confirmed, hopping to his feet and walking to the door.

"So, he gets to get out of here, but we don't," she said, sadly looking at the door as he escaped.

"Only for a little while longer, only to keep you safe," Nate reminded her. "You can handle it that long."

She nodded. "I can. It's just very frustrating."

He smiled. "It's all frustrating, but that doesn't mean it's any less important to follow safety guidelines."

"And yet we already know that the smugglers managed to find where we were before, so what's to say that they won't find us again?"

"No way to know," Nate admitted, "but our odds are better if we stay out of sight. Thus, we'll stay here, safe and sound, at least for now, and hopefully that won't happen."

"Sure," she muttered. "That all *sounds* good, but …"

"I can bring in coffee, if you want," Nate offered.

"No, Brody didn't want us to do room service. Did this room come with any single-serving coffee pods?"

He got up and looked in the kitchenette. "I found one. Do you want it?"

"Sure, or we can split it."

He shook his head. "I'm fine without it, or I might even have tea. I see some tea is here." She started to giggle. "What? Can't a guy have tea?" he asked in faux outrage.

She smiled. "Sure, you can. It just seems to be an odd choice for you."

"It shouldn't be, and don't stereotype me," he teased.

"In this line of work, we eat when we find food. So I enjoy a cup of tea once in a while."

"I do too," she admitted, still grinning. "What kind is there?" And with that they got into a discussion on the various teas, and he was happy that she at least got her mind off everything for a few minutes. Still, he knew it would be harder to keep her contained as the days went by. He felt as if they should probably change locations again soon, a thought that was reinforced when Brody abruptly came through the door, his expression hard.

CHAPTER 11

MADELINE HOPPED TO her feet, already concerned. "You don't have food, and you look pissed off. What happened?"

He frowned at her. "I don't know about *pissed off*," he replied, "but pack up. We're moving."

She groaned, but obediently headed to the bedroom and quickly grabbed her bag.

When she stepped out again, Brody noted, "That was fast."

"I don't unpack anymore. I'm a fast learner," she said.

And, with that, Brody led them outside their room and across the hallway to another room. She stared at the guys. "Why here?"

"Because we'll set a trap," Brody whispered.

"Okay. … What trap?"

"You'll stay here, in this new room, with one of us, while the other one of us will be in our registered room," Brody shared in a determined voice.

Nate nodded. "Obviously you have some intel."

"Not really, but I *was* followed." And, with that, he quickly disappeared into their old room. She looked at Nate as he closed and locked the door of their new room. She sat down hard on the nearest chair. "But that means he's a target now?"

"Maybe so, but trust me that he knows how to handle it," he told her. "Don't even begin to start worrying about him."

"Of course I'll worry about him. He's only in there because of the pickle I'm in," she stated. "It always makes me angry when other people have to step up and do something that I can't, putting their own lives in danger."

"Has it happened often?" Nate asked, that humorous tone back in his voice again.

She shrugged, then shook her head, frustrated. "No, it hasn't, but it doesn't make me feel any better."

He flashed her a big grin. "You might want to just go into your bedroom and lie down for a bit."

At that, she glared at him again. "No, I really don't want to."

He shrugged. "That's fine, but I don't know what'll happen here in the next few minutes."

"Will you stay right here the whole time?" she asked, chewing on her bottom lip.

"Yes, I will." When he perked up and quickly moved to the door, he placed his ear against it, holding a finger to his lips.

She quietly raced to his side and heard voices on the other side of the door.

He gave her a hard look, then pointed to a position behind the door. "Stay here and back out of sight," he whispered. Then he pulled open the door and stepped out into the hallway, for all the world to see, as if he were just some guest at the hotel. When he shut the door behind him, she paced the small hotel room, wondering what she could do.

Then she remembered that she wasn't powerless at all

and filled the hallway outside her door with warm, comforting happiness. She didn't know who was out there. It could have just been hotel staff for all she knew, but it wouldn't hurt anybody to feel happier.

When the door opened a few minutes later, Nate stuck his head around the door and looked at her quizzically. "You want to knock that off?"

She frowned. "Knock what off?"

"All that *happy-go-lucky* stuff."

She walked toward him and asked, "Why?"

"Because these guys are just laughing at every question we ask them, as if it's the biggest joke in the world."

She beamed. "So, it does work."

"Yeah, maybe too well," he stated, staring at her. "We are trying to interrogate them."

When she stepped out in the hallway, the bad guys continued to laugh and laugh and laugh.

"Hey," she greeted them, giving them a big bright smile. "I guess your boss won't be too happy if you don't find the second diamond stash, *huh*?" One of the men just waved his hand. "Doesn't matter. It's all good."

"If it's all good, why are you here then?"

He looked at her and shrugged. "Just following orders."

"Okay, and obedience goes that far?"

He gave her a benevolent smile, as if she didn't understand the ways of the world, and then he laughed. "Absolutely. The punishment is pretty steep if we don't."

She winced at that. "So, maybe you guys shouldn't be quite so happy about this job then?"

He chuckled again. "No, it's all good." He turned to his buddy and asked, "What shall we tell him?"

"That we were here and that the room was empty," he

said, with a shrug.

His partner agreed. "That sounds good to me."

She nodded. "I like that idea too. But maybe you should let us walk away first, give us a head start. Then you can tell him, and it will be true."

The two men nodded, as one spoke. "Good idea. Why don't you guys head on out? You won't be here, and it'll be all good."

She smiled, stepped back inside, grabbed her bag and Nate's too. She handed his to him, just as Brody joined them with his bag too. She told the two bad guys, "I really appreciate that you guys are happy to let us go. So I have a tip for you. I think the second stash of diamonds is in the Uber vehicle that Anna escaped in. Only the driver is dead, so I don't know where his car is," she shared, with a lovely and hopefully persuasive suggestion. As the men continued to beam at her, she patted one on the cheek and then the other. "I really do thank you. You guys are good at heart."

At that, Nate grabbed her by the arm and pulled her along.

With a big happy smile, she waved at the bad guys and hurried off behind Nate. As they reached the fire escape stairs, he bolted down, half dragging her with him.

"You really don't trust, do you?" she asked, scrambling to keep up.

"Hell no. You do know that their true natures will assert themselves very quickly, right?"

"Maybe, but I'm hoping that we can get far enough away before that happens."

"Yeah, I get that's what you're trying for," Nate said, "but it's a hell of a time to experiment. You did see that they were armed, right?"

Her heart started to beat faster in her chest, as she whispered, "No, I didn't."

"They didn't come just to check if we were here," he stated. "They came to take you out. That is a whole different story now and a pretty dicey game. Now if they go back to their boss and the job isn't done, they'll know perfectly well that something went wrong, and these guys will likely get shot."

She turned, then looked at him in horror. "That's why I told them about the stash."

"Yeah, and what if the diamonds aren't there? Just forget it. Don't worry about them. They were paid to take you out."

"But they could make a new decision and do what's right," she said.

"They could, but that's not likely to be the best decision for them. As far as their bosses go, either they die or you do."

She winced at that. "Right, I guess that's what Terkel and you two have been saying about not being responsible for everyone else and their decisions."

"Exactly. I'm glad you're getting that message."

She rolled her eyes at him. "I'm not dense. I would just prefer that the world be a happier place."

"So, you're doing everything you can to make it a happier place, and I get that. It's very commendable," he shared. "Yet haven't you heard that saying? Some proverb about trust in God but tie up the camel anyway? Meaning the prayers may work, but we still need to kick ass and to get the hell out of here."

CHAPTER 12

O UTSIDE, THE TRIO headed to one of the more public areas of town. When Nate shared a knowing look with Brody, he nodded. "I'm grabbing a car. We need a set of wheels."

When he had gone, Madeline turned to Nate. "Do you think we should tell the detective?"

"Yeah, we should." He quickly pulled out his phone and brought the detective up to speed.

"I'm downtown right now," the detective replied. "Where are you?"

He gave him the nearest intersection as a landmark.

"Okay, stay there. I'll be there in a minute."

Nate then texted Brody and let him know. When Brody walked over to rejoin them a few minutes later, he asked, "Are you sure about this? And did you tell Manshue bout Madeline's idea where the second stash could be?"

Nate nodded. "We have to trust somebody," Nate conceded, "and, with Madeline here along for the ride, we might survive this craziness."

Brody turned to her and shook his head. "That happiness energy of yours *was* crazy. I've never seen anything like it."

"It's a good thing that you get to see it now," she said, with a bright smile in his direction. "It was hard to keep my true personality quiet and content, when I didn't know what was going on. It's always a hardship that way."

"Yet now you're quite comfortable?" Brody asked, frowning.

"Yes, because at least you guys are okay with it," she pointed out. "I didn't want anybody knowing what I was doing, so that hampered my ability to do anything. Weird how that works."

"It works that way all the time," Nate stated, with a smile, "and it's an adjustment, no matter who you are with. You will always be adjusting to different energies."

"Ah, so maybe that's why it's so easy with you guys because your energy gets along with mine. Plus, you're just nice guys." Brody shot her a hard look, and she gave him an impudent grin in return. "I can't wait to meet your wife and to tell her what a nice person you are."

He groaned and rolled his eyes. "Yeah, she won't believe you."

"Sure, she will. I'll explain it to her," Madeline shared, with a casual wave of her hand.

When the detective pulled up a few minutes later, they got into the back of his vehicle.

Manshue looked at them suspiciously. "I don't know how you guys keep evading these attacks, but I'm grateful that you have. And I appreciate the theory on where the second stash may be, no matter how outlandish is sounds. The sting is in play right now, so hopefully it'll come to pass within the next few hours, and we'll have every known associate rounded up."

"That would be lovely," she said, beaming at him. "And then I want to go home."

"Right, and where's home again?"

"It'll be Manchester, even if I haven't lived there before."

He shot her a look. "Okay."

She just smiled and didn't elaborate. As they drove forward, she asked him, "Where are we going now?"

"To another safe house, though you guys are exposing our safe houses."

"That's okay. You can use them again later."

He laughed. "As long as nobody knows where they are and that they haven't been compromised, sure. But it's troublesome that those safe houses and the hotels you guys have been at were found out in fairly short order by the smuggling ring. That's a problem."

"Yeah, because somebody on the inside is feeding them information," Nate declared from the back seat.

The detective looked at him in the rearview mirror. "What do you mean?"

"I think you have a dirty cop in the mix," Nate replied. "Somebody in your organization is passing along that information and is part of the smuggling ring."

The detective shook his head. "Hell no, no way, they wouldn't dare. The punishment for that thing over here is too harsh, too extreme."

"I doubt it," Nate argued, "although I have heard some unpleasant things. It's still a case of what works, and most people are greedy enough to believe they can get out of it, no matter what."

"That would be foolish of them if that's the case," the detective added, his gaze going from one of them to the other. "I can't imagine anybody trying it."

"Maybe not," Nate conceded, "but I can't think of any other reason that anybody would know where we are all the time."

"Did you check for trackers?" he asked.

"Manually, yes. Brody and I are not tracked, and Madeline couldn't find anything on her. So, unless she was injected with something, … but that would mean the ring must be pretty sophisticated."

"Yeah, and what about the millions of dollars moving contraband across borders? Isn't that sophisticated enough for you?" the detective asked.

Madeline frowned at Nate, a question in her eyes, and he just shrugged.

As the detective drove along a little bit farther, she looked around. "What section of town is this?"

"I'm coming up to our safe place, right up ahead." The detective took a series of quick sharp turns, then pulled into a loading bay at the back of a warehouse. It was pretty dark here, and he shut off the engine. Almost immediately the car doors were unlocked, and he opened up his door. "Come on. Let's go."

Before she had a chance to do anything, all three of the other doors were opened from the outside, and she gasped as she stared at the face of the man that she had changed seats with on the plane. "Well, shit," she muttered, "that didn't go so well."

NOW INSIDE THE warehouse, Nate had half expected the trap and was really hoping she was as good with that happiness energy thing as she seemed to be with the first two gunmen because, right about now, they faced four gunmen and would need that inside help to even the odds. He glared at the four men holding guns on them, then at the detective.

"We wondered if it was you."

The detective ignored him, instead addressing the head gunman. "I don't know that she knows anything. As I told you before, we found the diamonds at the morgue."

"Yeah, but we didn't get all of them," he snapped, "so somebody has the others."

"I don't know anything about those, but she has a wild imagination and thinks the second stash is in the car of the dead driver," the detective stated. "That's pure speculation on her part, but your men and mine both know. So go find them. Regardless she doesn't know anything about your smuggling ring either."

"Yet you still brought her."

"Sure, because you made it very clear what would happen if I didn't," he replied, followed by a dark growl. "It's bad enough that you've already brought me in this much."

It was obvious that the detective was quite pissed, but something was off about his energy too. Nate didn't know what the hell was going on. He looked at Brody, who had an odd look on his face, as he studied the gunman in front of him. Brody seemed to be projecting a taunt, *Go ahead, shoot me, and see what it will get you.* Nate didn't know what Brody had in terms of energy skills, but, with these guys of Terk's, anything was possible.

"I told you that I had nothing to do with it," the detective repeated.

"Yeah, sure you did," the head gunman agreed. "Yet we can't trust you cops."

"Of course not," the detective replied. "You know that our job is to bring you guys in."

"That won't happen. We need to take out these guys who stole from us and close that loop," the head man stated.

"We probably won't be back in your country again for a while anyway."

Nate thought he discerned an odd Russian overtone to the head guy's words, but then again what did Nate know? He wasn't very good with accents. He looked over at Brody, who still hadn't moved. Nate's gaze went from one gunman to the other, surprised when the detective stepped back.

"Now I get to leave?" Manshue asked.

"That's what you thought?" the boss man quipped. "How *perceptive*."

"Wait, you told me this would be it."

"Sure, I told you that, but obviously we can't let you walk away," he muttered in disgust. "We want our diamonds back. What kind of a fool are you?"

"He's a good man," Madeline spoke up. "You really shouldn't hurt him."

"Really? He betrayed you."

"Did he?" she asked, studying the head gunman, then the detective. She returned her gaze to the boss man. "I think *betrayal* is a harsh word right now."

The gunman snorted. "Who are you kidding? How about you just shut up and look like the pretty bitch you are."

She frowned at him, and genuine hurt filled her gaze. "I really don't like it when people talk to me like that."

He snorted. "I'll talk to you any way I want, and, if you don't shut up, it'll be a hell of a lot worse for you," he warned. "Matter of fact, I think I'll just shut you up now." He took a threatening step toward her.

At once her jaw clenched. "I learned to stand up to bullies a long time ago, and that's what you are, just a bully."

Nate placed a hand on her shoulder.

The head guy laughed. "Yeah, you better shut her up," the boss man declared. "I don't know what her problem is, but if she thinks talking back to me will get her anywhere, she's wrong."

"I don't think she's trying to talk back to you, honestly," Nate explained. "She's built different that way."

She turned and glared at Nate. "Are you saying something's wrong with me?"

He laughed. "No, definitely not. Something is absolutely *very right* about you."

She gave him a beaming smile, and he watched the waves of energy coming off her, as she worked on her nice approach to the head guy with the gun. Yet Nate could also see that it would be a very hard sell. This guy had absolutely no give in his soul, and somebody like that would not be easy for her to apply her happiness energy.

She looked over at the detective. "You must be sorry that you ever got involved in this."

He disagreed. "I didn't get involved. These guys threatened me and my family. I had no choice when it comes down to that. And I am sorry. I would have done a lot to avoid getting you into trouble, but my family …"

"I understand. Family is family. You've been through enough, and thank you for that." She nodded. "I personally agree with you about family. I also think these guys should stop smuggling and kidnapping."

"Isn't that nice," quipped the gunman assigned to her, who had remained silent up until now. "Yet it really doesn't matter what you think."

"No," she conceded, with an assessing look. "And you're the kind of guy who shoots first and asks questions later, aren't you?"

"Well, you're still alive, so apparently not," he said, then gave a reckless laugh.

"You're also the kind of guy who very much wants to be the boss of his outfit and to not take any more orders from this asshole beside you."

Shocked, the second gunman turned to look at his boss, who was staring at him.

"Is she right?" the boss asked. "Did you tell her that? Have you been bitching about taking orders from me?"

"What the hell?" gunman number two replied. "How could I possibly have talked to her? She's just trying to get your goat."

"She got it all right," he snapped, glaring at his righthand man. "You know how I feel about people trying to get one up on me, and I really don't appreciate it when people try to take over my position," he muttered in a deadly calm manner. "You know what happened to the last guy who tried to get the jump on me, right?"

The other gunman paled. "I wouldn't do that. We've worked together for a very long time," he reminded his boss. "Don't let her get to you like this, man."

At that, the boss man glared at him and raised his gun. "I don't know what's going on here or why all of a sudden I'm seeing you clearly for the first time. However, it just occurred to me that this is all about you working your way up the ladder, and me taking the fall at some point in time, likely with a knife in my back. You prefer those close-encounter assassinations, don't you?"

The gunman stared at him in shock. "I don't know what brought this on, but I haven't done anything to you."

"No, but you were thinking about it," Madeline declared. "You've been thinking about it a lot. Now this is a good opportunity for a step up in the organization, isn't it? There'll be a lot of dead bodies, after all. The whole thing will blow up, and you could blame your boss, then move nicely into his position. You are next in line, right? So really, how could you *not* think about it?"

Nate wasn't at all sure what game she was playing, but he knew that Brody was waiting for something, anything, that would allow them to take over. That turning point wouldn't be all that long at the rate that she was stirring the pot here. Nate wasn't sure whether he should smile at her and cheer her on, or tell her to watch out because each of these gunmen were as unpredictable as rattlesnakes.

CHAPTER 13

MADELINE FOUND IT hard to keep an eye on all four gunmen and also carefully stir the pot, yet not cross the line with her use of energy. Still, Brody and Nate were waiting for something, any opportunity for them to gain the upper hand. But she didn't want them getting hurt; she didn't want anything to happen to them.

Now the four gunmen were a whole different story. She knew it would be pretty easy for her to turn into that person she didn't want to be, and yet they had forced the detective into this, at least he said they had. However, something else was going on here, and she didn't quite understand it. The energy flowed at a rate that just astonished her. It was moving so quickly that she couldn't even see it.

The boss man was much stronger than she'd expected, and he was resisting her happiness mojo, which is why she had decided to uncover how his righthand man was against him, hoping to give them an opportunity to bite in any direction. So far, it seemed to be working, but she didn't understand all the energy here. She'd had no time to even assimilate and analyze it, and she wasn't very good at that anyway. She was very much more the *jump in with both feet and get the job done* type. Plus, she was the newbie here, which caused her a little concern at the moment.

She turned to the third gunman, just silently standing

here, staring at them. "Look at you," she said, with a nod. "You're just waiting to see where the dust settles, aren't you?"

He gave her a lazy smile. "Why not?" he asked. "People change all the time. So I'll just sit back and watch it happen."

"What about us?" she asked, hoping this laidback gunman's energy was a little more open and sustainable. Yet, as she tried to send some of her happiness energy in his direction, it was rebuffed, and she knew that her efforts to convince him would not happen.

What people were these that they chose to live in such darkness?

"I'm so sorry for you," she said gently. "That dark world you live in must be very hard to deal with on a daily basis."

He shot her a look and snorted. "I don't know what glue you're sniffing, but your wiles won't work on me."

"What wiles?" she asked in bewilderment. "I'm just wondering how unhappy your childhood must have been that this is the job you end up in. What kind of a life can you have if you're here waiting to see if your top two bosses will fight it out against each other, wondering who'll win?" She looked back at the top two men, who were still glaring at each other.

"I didn't do anything," number two declared to the boss man, "and you know it."

"No, I don't know it," the head gunman snapped. "For all I know, you're behind all this. Where are my diamonds?" he yelled.

Eyebrows up in shock, the number two man shook his head, "I'm behind you, that's what. I came here with you to take them down, and, instead of doing our jobs, we're sitting here, arguing, as if we're two kids in a sandbox. And still no confirmation on the second stash."

She wouldn't say anything to that because it was a little too apropos, but the third gunman laughed out loud.

"That's a good point," he agreed. "Maybe we should take care of these four civilians before we air any more vital information, while we hang out our dirty laundry," he said, sweeping his gun over the four of them.

"Why me?" the detective asked bitterly.

She looked at him, wondering if he really believed that he should be selfishly set free. When she noted something was behind his ear, along with his previous message about a sting being put in place, then it hit her. She turned to Brody and Nate. They didn't quite understand what was going on, but they understood that something was up. So they were just playing along and waiting, ever ready.

And that's what she wasn't—she wasn't ready. She didn't know what was coming down the pipeline, and, while she wanted to be ready, that wasn't the easiest thing for her. This event was not in her life experience. She looked from one gunman to the other. "Could you guys move along and just solve this, please? Go check out the Uber car for the missing diamonds. I really want to see how it plays out."

The boss man snorted. "You started this, and I'm not too interested in playing a game just for your amusement." He turned and lifted his handgun at her, but she just gave him the sweetest smile. He slowly lowered his gun, frowning. "Are you a fool? What the hell is that for?"

"What's what?" she asked.

"You're smiling at me, almost as if you're thanking me," he replied in bewilderment. "Something is very off about you, woman."

"Yeah, I've heard that a time or two," she stated, with a

sad smile. "But when you just want to be a nice person, the world isn't always terribly friendly to you."

"This is a *kill or be killed* world," the third gunman noted.

Then Number Two frowned at him. "And yet we've always gotten along just fine, … up until now."

"Yeah, it's the *up until now* part that makes me wonder," said the boss man. "I think you've just been biding your time." Then, without any warning, he lifted his gun and shot his number two, dropping the poor man to the ground instantly.

She gasped in horror, shocked to see the blood welling from the man's chest.

She wanted to run over and drop to his side to help him, but Nate gripped her hand tighter and pulled her even closer to his side. She heard him, his tone hard and reverberating through her head, almost creating a headache with the force of his delivery, as he said, *NO.*

Her breath shuddered in her chest, and the tears welled up, as she glanced from one gunman to the other. "What monsters you are," she declared, "that you would shoot one of your own, when he did absolutely nothing?"

"He would try to take over my position," the boss man decreed. He looked over at his number three. "You got any arguments?"

The man shrugged. "Hell no, you and I already discussed that he would probably pull this one day, so it makes sense," he said. "Now, can we just shoot these four, go find the diamonds, and get the hell out of France? I get the feeling we can't be here much longer."

"Yeah, me too," the boss man stated. "We would have been done and gone except for this."

Then he raised his gun and turned it in her direction. Madeline sucked back her breath, sending out as much love as she possibly could, even in the face of all that hatred.

All of a sudden, brilliant lights turned on all around them, and she heard shouts, loud and clear.

"Police, hands up!"

NATE SHOOK THE detective's hand. "It would have been nice if you'd let us in on the plan."

"Yeah, it would have, if I could have," he muttered. "My bosses were totally against it. They figured that since you guys were being found all the time, we should let them find you, which was literally the last part of the trap they were setting to make this all go down, and, for that, I'm really sorry."

She looked at him in shock. "You deliberately led us here as part of your plan to pick them up?"

He nodded. "Not my plan though," he repeated apologetically. "This is one of those times when you don't agree with what the bosses are doing, but you understand and hope for the best." He shrugged, "For that, I can't do anything but apologize because they're way above me in the pay grade and pecking order."

She looked over at Nate, who stared at the detective, with fury in his gaze, but she also knew that it was more about her being put in that precarious position. She walked over and smiled up at him. "I'm fine, you know."

He looked down at her, and his shoulders sagged, and he snatched her into his arms and crushed her against his chest. She smiled, and he leaned over and kissed her. "You are fine," he noted, glaring at the detective, "but they could have done this sting without you."

"And yet this way, it's over, it's done, and now we can leave." She turned and glared at the detective, almost afraid to hear his answer. "Right? Particularly after that stunt you just pulled," she added. "If you dare say no, believe me that I'll have the media all over this."

He smiled. "It is among the conditions I made that, after this sting, you are to be released and are no longer under suspicion. Yet we still have quite a few other members of the ring to pick up." Just then his phone rang, and while he answered it, they watched. When he got off the call, he gave a nod of satisfaction. "So, the sweep is complete, and we've picked up fourteen more members," he shared, with a big smile. "And I'm surprised to report that the diamonds were found in the Uber driver's car. And I thought you just told the gunmen that to let you go earlier. Also we did find a rat on the force. He is behind bars. And while I don't understand the dirty cop, I really don't know exactly what happened back there"—he pointed, turning to look at the dead man on the warehouse floor, still lying in front of them—"yet it worked. So for that I'm grateful. Now I have to leave." Hesitating, he added, "Do you guys need a ride to the airport?"

"No, we'll be fine," Brody replied. "Believe me that we won't be taking any rides from you again."

The detective flushed and then, shamefaced, replied in an apologetic tone, "I can understand that." And, with that, he was gone.

Nate looked over at Brody. "How quickly can we get flights out of here?"

"I already sent Terkel a message. As soon as we hear back

from him, and we collect her passport, and our gear, we can go."

"Why don't we just head to the airport, make the necessary stops as we go, and hopefully we'll hear along the way," she muttered. "I want to get the hell away from here."

Nate noted that she carefully avoided looking at the dead body on the ground. "Remember," he whispered. "You're not responsible." But he caught the sheen of tears in her eyes, and he wrapped an arm around her and tucked her up closer. "Come on. Let's get to the airport."

With that, they headed outside to grab a taxi. However, a private car pulled up in front of them. The driver stepped out and walked right up to Nate and Brody and Madeline. "I'm Garret, Bullard's man. I've missed the whole op, it seems, due to technical issues with my flights and then MI6 issues." He gave a laugh. "So the least I can do it give you a ride to the airport."

They all shared a good laugh and updated Garret on the op, thanking him for all his troubles in getting here.

"We do appreciate your efforts to help us," Nate added, as they all piled into Garret's vehicle.

After picking up their gear, and a quick stop at the consulate for her passport, Terkel redirected them to a small private airport, where Garret dropped them off. A small plane sat on the tarmac and had just finished its safety check. They boarded and were quickly in the air.

Madeline sank into the comfy seat. "I am so glad that's over. I still can't believe the detective was part of the sting."

"We also would have preferred that he didn't use you as bait," Brody began, "so it'll be a long cold day before I trust anybody in the French police department, yet I understand why they did it."

"I understand it too," she muttered, "but I sure don't appreciate being the bait *or* the patsy."

He smiled at her. "But whatever you did with the gunmen was also a pretty neat trick," he muttered. "And that makes me a little wary of you too."

She stared at him and shook her head. "I didn't do anything. I was trying to influence them to do good, but I couldn't make nice things happen with those four gunmen," she admitted. "Their hearts and souls were too far gone, I guess. So the only thing I could think of was to sow the seeds of doubt instead, taking whatever was already on their minds and empowering it. I didn't have anything to do with creating that tension because that was already in the one guy's mind," she noted sadly. "It just seems to be the world that these bad guys live in."

"Absolutely," Brody agreed, with a smile. "And it's good to know you can do that. However, you don't realize what a drain on your body you are causing when you send out this *be nice* energy all day long. So just ration that and a lot of your hunger and tired issues will wane. You'll learn more about that with Terk to help you. Plus, you'll have a lot of fun at the castle, learning how to do even more cool stuff. You can try to teach us your tricks as well."

"Maybe," she muttered, "but I'm also pretty tired and just need some time to unwind."

"So does that mean you don't want to go to the castle right away?" Nate asked.

She winced. "Sort of, but, if that means going somewhere else, I'm not up for that either. I just want to get home and to stay there. No more traveling."

Nate grabbed her hand. "I vote for the castle," he replied, "especially if we have private quarters."

She looked up at him and frowned. "I didn't even think about that."

"And that's fine because we are both learning more about Terk and his headquarters and about the energy work," he noted comfortably. "You and I both know where we're heading. We'll just take our time getting there."

She smiled. "Do you think it works like that?"

"It works any way we want it to work," he said. "However, it'll be very overwhelming when we get there. Remember all those people and the pregnant women? So you'll need to be nice."

She snorted. "Really? Is that me who you're telling to be nice? When am I ever *not* nice?"

"When you're pitting one gunman against another," he pointed out, with a chuckle.

Sure enough, when they landed, a large SUV waited for them. As she got into the back, Brody greeted somebody else as if long-lost friends.

"They really are part of a team, like a family even," she told Nate. "It'll be hard to be on the outside."

"No," Nate disagreed, "it won't. You will only be on the outside until you feel as if you're part of them," he explained, looking at her with a gentle smile. "And I have a hunch that won't take very long."

She hoped so. By the time she met everybody and was shown to one wing of the castle, her head was reeling to the point of pain. She was intent on just lying down.

Terkel stopped her in front of one of the doors in this hallway. "I know what is happening here."

"You do?"

"Yeah, you aren't used to this much energy consolidated into one space," he told her. "So you'll feel as if you've been given a knockout pill for a while. Just take it easy and give yourself the next few days to slowly assimilate. Then, as you get used to being around all these energy workers, we'll teach you how to put up some guards so you're not so overwhelmed."

"Great, sounds good. I just need to lie down right now though."

"Good idea. Nate's looking for you as well."

"Tell him where I am then," she muttered, yawning. "Whatever it is about this place, it's overwhelming."

"Don't worry about that," Terk reassured her, "not yet, not right now. It's all too much to begin with, but you'll settle in and find your place."

She smiled. "Thank you."

He leaned over and gave her a big hug. "Go get some rest." With that, he opened the door, and she stepped into the apartment, only to find Nate there, lying on the bed, waiting for her.

"Hey," he said, getting up. "How are you doing?"

"I'm okay, … just a little overwhelmed." Her mind went into overdrive, thinking about all the women she just met, all the very large pregnant bellies at various stages all around her. "However, this is a fascinating place."

"Full of joy, full of life, full of hope," he noted.

Considering that gave her an emotional boost, and she beamed at Nate. "You are so correct there. I've never seen anything like it."

"And probably never will again," he said, with a chuckle. "And that's not bad. It just is what it is. It's how it is, and that's good for us, right? Now, as for that headache of yours, come on down here, and let's see if I can get rid of it."

"What will you do?" she asked, followed by a yawn.

"A massage might help," he suggested. "You've been pretty tense for quite a while."

"I met a lot of people," she said, "a lot of strangers who don't really know me."

"Yet they know *of* you, and they know what you did because Brody told them."

She winced. "That's not necessarily a good thing, though."

"Yes, it is." Nate took her hand. "Everybody here accepts you for who you are and for what you can do. That is the gift that being one of Terkel's team gives you, and it's one you can cherish."

She smiled as she crashed on the bed beside him. "So, tell me. How come we have an apartment together?"

"Because when Terkel asked if we needed one or two, I told him one."

She rolled onto her back and looked at him. "You did mention something about that earlier."

"We also discussed how we needed time and some space, and the only way we'll get that is if we have some privacy," he reminded her. "So, if you don't want this arrangement, we can change it, whether in a week, a day, tomorrow, tonight, whenever and whatever you want. Right now you just need to get some rest."

She closed her eyes, and he slowly worked on the muscles along her back and shoulders. Just before she slipped off to sleep, she whispered, "Will you be here when I wake up?"

He leaned over and asked, "Do you want me to be?"

She smiled. "Yes, please."

"Then I will."

With that, she closed her eyes and crashed.

NATE HAD TO admit that Madeline had handled herself very well, considering all she'd been through. Coming to Terk's castle had been a tumultuous arrival in its own right, with Brody arriving home safe and sound to his family, plus two new members for the team in tow, both energy workers. Madeline even got to talk to Bullard on the phone, thanking him for starting the search for her and apologizing for not wanting to travel to Africa, even for him. He was very gracious and totally understood. Still, he extended her an open invitation to visit his compound, when her fear of traveling was gone. She had to laugh at that.

Brody had clearly shared something about what Madeline could do, and that had raised the eyebrows of most of the women, but they were thoroughly in love with the whole concept of niceness and the use of her energy in such a unique way. Nate knew it was useless to argue the idea of somebody having that much influence on people. He had certainly seen way too much of the ugliness of life, so he was all for the idea of spending time getting comfortable with the good energies in life. This was just another example.

He dozed off beside Madeline several times himself, knowing it would be a few days before they had a chance to adapt to the chaos of this much energy in one place, before they had a chance to begin to unwind.

When he woke up the next time, Madeline stood over him, looking to see if he was awake. He blinked, and she made a startled sound and stepped back.

He chuckled. "I'm awake. I just thought that, if you were sleeping, I would doze a bit too."

She smiled. "Thank you for staying with me while I

slept. I do feel better."

"Good. Me too."

"But I'm still hesitant to go out and face the music. A lot of people are in Terkel's little piece of the world."

"Indeed, and honestly, there's no rush," he told her. "We can stay here and just spend some time together, if you want."

"Does that mean we have room service?"

"Uh, no. It does not," he said, laughing. "But I do understand that, while meals are made to have together in one of the dining rooms, everybody doesn't have to partake. People are free to do whatever they want. I just don't know all the details, but I'll figure out the system soon enough."

"No," she said, placing a finger against his lips. "*We* will figure out the system soon enough, and, though I'm not all that good at it," she shared, "I do love to cook."

"If you ever want to take over and cook a meal, I don't think anybody here would argue with you for taking that off their hands."

She laughed. "But I don't know if my nursing skills are needed here."

"Did you see all those pregnant bellies out there?" he asked, mock horror in his gaze.

"So who was the guy getting off another plane when we got in?"

"*Ah*, that was Riff," Nate said. "He was coming back from some personal visit in America."

"A very strange energy comes from him."

"Yeah, if you can get him to be friendly and to open up, apparently that would be a miracle."

She smiled. "He's a teddy bear inside," she revealed, yawning. "He's just hurting, and, as soon as that hurt eases back some, he'll be fine." At Nate's expression of curiosity, she shrugged. "It's not my story to tell, but I can feel his pain. Better yet, I can heal that pain." She looked around, deliberately avoiding Nate's gaze. "Although Riff won't necessarily be terribly interested in doing that."

"Why is that?" Nate asked.

"It's that whole matter of pride. He feels guilty. Something happened, and he thinks it's his fault. So, until he can solve it or absolve himself of whatever he believes he did wrong, he'll be this way," she shared. Then, as if trying to shake herself out of that mental scene, she focused on Nate. "How about a shower?"

"A shower would be good." He nodded. "You can go ahead first. The towels are in there."

She smiled but shook her head. "Good, but how about a shower together?"

He raised an eyebrow. "Oh," he said, a big grin on his face. "That sounds perfect." He watched in amazement as she stripped down to her bare skin, and, with no sign of self-consciousness, walked her long, lean body to the bathroom. She turned at the doorway. "Two big towels are here. Are you coming?"

He gave her a goofy grin. "I was just admiring the view."

She rolled her eyes. "Here I thought you would have already raced in ahead of me."

At that, he started stripping down and had his clothes off as quickly as possible.

She nodded when she saw his heavily muscled body. "I do like your muscles." She gave a contented sigh, sliding a finger over his abs. His muscles clenched tightly in response, and she chuckled. "You're ticklish."

"Am not."

But of course he was, and she knew there would be hell to pay when he found her own ticklish spots. She flashed him a bright smirk and turned on the hot water. She stepped into the huge shower, definitely big enough for two, and waited for him to join her. "This is incredible."

"It is," he agreed. "Even comes with a bench, if you get tired or want to sit."

She sat down and nodded. "This is something else I like too." She snatched the shampoo and went to work on her hair. He pulled her to stand with her back to his chest and gave her a deep scalp massage, working in the shampoo, then rinsed it all out, picked up the conditioner, and did the same thing. She leaned back against him, her body warm and flushed from the heat of the water. "You're really good at this."

"That's a surprise," he noted, "considering that I've never done it before." She opened her eyes and turned to look at him. He nodded and added, "It makes a difference when it's somebody you care about."

She kissed him gently. "Absolutely."

By the time he was done with her hair, she had a bar of soap in hand to work on his body. It was one thing to keep his reaction down while he had been working on her hair, but it was another thing entirely when her soapy hands slipped over his wet body.

She chuckled when he rose to the occasion. "Not sure I want our first time to be in the shower," she shared, looking up at him from her seat on the bench. "Yet I'm sure getting lots of ideas for future visits."

By the time they were both soaped and rinsed, he turned off the shower, his erection tormenting him heavily. He knew that he was in danger of taking her right here in the shower, with absolutely no finesse, reacting to her words as she kept up a running commentary about his body.

He wrapped her up in a towel, then quickly dried himself off as much as he could in three short strokes. He scooped her up in his arms, towel and all, and, ignoring her shriek of laughter, tossed her gently on the bed and followed her down.

She opened her arms wide. "So, not in the shower?"

"Only because it wasn't your preference for our first time, but maybe next time."

"Or the time after," she murmured, her tongue sliding deep into his mouth, warring with his.

When he could breathe again, he dropped his forehead to hers and whispered, "You are amazing."

"Oh, I don't know about that," she murmured, as she stretched out beneath him. "I do love this though."

He chuckled and kissed her gently, leaving a trail of kisses down her throat and across one plump breast, taking the nipple gently in his mouth. She arched beneath him, responsive like he'd never seen before as she twisted beneath him, her hands frantically raking through the curls on his head.

"It's the energy," she muttered. "It's got to be the energy, but I want you now, and I don't think I can wait."

Surprised, but more than capable of taking his cue from her, he rested at the heart of her, as she wrapped her thighs around him, impaling herself on his shaft as she cried out and arched again beneath him.

Enchanted at her completely natural response, he quickly encircled one nipple and then the other with his mouth, while his hands gripped her buttocks. He tucked her up tightly against him, only to shift his position and slowly start to move. In one of his hands, he grabbed both of hers and placed them over her head, her arms stretched out. Then using the headboard for support with his free hand, he slowly drove deeper and deeper into her. When she convulsed beneath him, it was music to his ears, as she did it again and then again.

By the time he collapsed on top of her, his own climax ripping through him, her body released one more time, and she fell into a sublime coma beside him. He rolled over, tucked her up close, and said, "I've never experienced that before."

"Me neither," she muttered, her tone drowsy. "That was the best thing ever. It's got to be the energy element."

He chuckled and gently nuzzled her neck. "You should get some sleep."

She opened her eyes, thought about it, and then nodded. "I can, can't I? … It's all over. We're here, safe and sound, and, even better, … we're together." With that she drifted off into a deep sleep.

He held her close, so thankful that they were safe, that they were together, and, with any luck at all, that they would be together forever. He never thought he would ever experience real love, and yet here he was, cheering it on with all his heart, hoping they could make this one dream come true for both of them. He smiled, kissed her gently on the cheek, and followed her down into the depths of sleep, with happy dreams rolling through his mind.

EPILOGUE

I N THE KITCHEN, seated among some other members of his team at the huge dining table, Terkel shuffled through the paperwork before him and still smiled when Natalia handed him a large accounting binder. He shoved it back at her. "Just give me the CliffsNotes version."

She laughed. "The CliffsNotes are in this binder," she stated. "That satellite is damn important to us."

"It is and it isn't," he replied. "The world's a mess, and we can use two satellites owned by our generous friends, but if one of them goes down—"

"I understand," she said, "so we need to keep working toward putting away funding for our own. So more jobs would be good."

He rolled his eyes at that. "We also need to sustain our ability to crew these ops, without sending everybody out on these jobs."

"Which we seem to be doing so far, especially with the help of Levi's and Bullard's teams," she noted, with a chuckle. "Other jobs are coming in, right?"

Terk nodded. "Actually a local job is next, but I'm not too sure how to handle it yet."

"Why is that?"

"It involves a woman with abilities I've talked to in the past. However, she's never been very up-front and open about joining our group. Yet she contacted me a few days ago and wants our help."

"What kind of help, and does she have money to pay us?"

He laughed. "She does have money. She was an influencer for a long time, made millions of dollars, then disappeared from public view. When I checked in on her, she told me that she was fine, yet she was putting off this *stay away* energy about her."

"What about now?" Clary asked, as she got up from the huge dining table to get more coffee and then moved closer to the discussion at hand. "It's always fascinating when a woman's involved."

"Lately it seems as if a woman is always involved," Terk stated, with a sigh. "It's that whole *Love Boat* thing going on again."

"I think you can blame Levi for that," Clary noted, with a laugh.

"Maybe." Terk grinned at the thought. "Anyway, her name is Janna, and her problem, at least according to her, is that somebody keeps contacting her that they need help, but she doesn't know where they are. Now it's gotten to the point where she can't function.

"Who is contacting Janna?"

"Somebody she used to know a long time ago. They were lovers for a while, and then he disappeared and went off into some military training. Something happened after that," he explained. "I'm waiting for the file to come in. I told her I wouldn't even look at it until I had more information, and she said she had no choice but to help as much as she could, since she knows him. Plus, he's locked on to her energy, and she hasn't been able to shake loose of him."

"She wants to shake loose?"

"She wants to, but I'm not exactly sure why. She's coming in today to talk to me."

"So, she is local?"

"She is."

At that, Sophia walked into the kitchen with a woman at her side. The visitor was dressed in jeans and a T-shirt, with a huge cardigan pulled up around her neck. She had masses of bright red hair, and scars on her lower left jaw and neck. She looked at Terkel expectantly.

Terkel stood up and studied her face. "Janna?"

She nodded slowly. "How can you even recognize me?" she asked bitterly. "Look at my face."

"I see your face," he stated, "and, yes, I've seen your previous photos as well. Why don't you tell me what happened."

She shrugged. "A fan found out where I lived and threw acid in my face," she shared. "I went underground and away from the world for a long time, right up until I started getting these calls." She sighed. "Calls I can no longer ignore."

Terk nodded. "Did you bring your information?"

She held out a folder and nodded. "This is all I have on him. His name is Royal Wilford. This holds all the information on his calls and everything on our history, plus anything else I could get my hands on."

He nodded and asked, "And you're prepared for whatever reception you get?"

"I don't have a choice," she admitted. "I already know what it's like for people to see my face and stare. If I could do anything more about it, I would, but I can't do a whole lot else. This is what I'm left with. Meanwhile, I can't leave him alone, so I have no choice but to come out of my safe and secluded existence and deal with it."

"Why is that?"

She frowned and looked down at her hands.

Terkel added, "We need to know, Janna."

"He was the father of my one and only child," she replied, her voice barely above a whisper, "who died of SIDs seven years ago. He didn't know there was a child, and he didn't know about our son's death either. I guess I feel as if I owe him. He gave me a wonderful gift, even if it was a gift I couldn't keep," she added, tears in her eyes.

"Go on."

"And now that he needs help, I can't just walk away."

"I get it," Terk replied, then looked over at the others gathered at the table. "Are you guys ready to take a look at this case?" They nodded, and, almost as if he'd made an announcement over a loudspeaker, more people started to filter into the massive dining room.

Janna stared in shock as more and more people gathered. "Terkel?"

"Yeah." He nodded, smiling with pride. "The team … grew."

"I guess that's a good thing?" she said doubtfully.

"It's a *great* thing," he declared, pulling out a chair for her. "Take a seat, and welcome to the family."

This concludes Book 8 of Terk's Guardians: Nate.
Read about Royal: Terk's Guardians, Book 9

Terk's Guardians: Royal (Book #9)

A prisoner of the Kremlin and of a failed exchange several years ago, Royal is losing hope of ever being free again—particularly when the firing squad date is already set for his execution. He has exhausted all avenues of escape. Now it seems to be the end of the line …

Janna has been through way-too-much pain and anguish recently, and yet somehow she can't walk away from helping Royal, even though he'd walked away from her a long time ago. Maybe because she has nothing left to care about, this would be her last gift to give—if someone can just get to Royal in time.

Time is against them. Conditions are against them. Enemies are against them. Can they fight the odds, and, in the process, save themselves?

Find Book 9 here!

To find out more visit Dale Mayer's website.

https://geni.us/DMSRoyal

Author's Note

Thank you for reading Nate: Terk's Guardians, Book 8! If you enjoyed the book, please take a moment and leave a short review.

Dear reader,

I love to hear from readers, and you can contact me at my website: www.dalemayer.com or at my Facebook author page. To be informed of new releases and special offers, sign up for my newsletter or follow me on BookBub. And if you are interested in joining Dale Mayer's Reader Group, here is the Facebook sign up page.
http://geni.us/DaleMayerFBGroup

Cheers,
Dale Mayer

About the Author

Dale Mayer is a *USA Today* best-selling author, best known for her SEALs military romances, her Psychic Visions series, and her Lovely Lethal Garden cozy series. Her contemporary romances are raw and full of passion and emotion (Broken But … Mending, Hathaway House series). Her thrillers will keep you guessing (Kate Morgan, By Death series), and her romantic comedies will keep you giggling (*It's a Dog's Life*, a stand-alone novella; and the Broken Protocols series, starring Charming Marvin, the cat).

Dale honors the stories that come to her—and some of them are crazy, break all the rules and cross multiple genres!

To go with her fiction, she also writes nonfiction in many different fields, with books available on résumé writing, companion gardening, and the US mortgage system. All her books are available in print and ebook format.

Connect with Dale Mayer Online

Dale's Website – www.dalemayer.com
Twitter – @DaleMayer
Facebook Page – geni.us/DaleMayerFBFanPage
Facebook Group – geni.us/DaleMayerFBGroup
BookBub – geni.us/DaleMayerBookbub
Instagram – geni.us/DaleMayerInstagram
Goodreads – geni.us/DaleMayerGoodreads
Newsletter – geni.us/DaleNews